The Case
of the Murdered
Players

BOOKS BY ROBERT NEWMAN

The Shattered Stone
Merlin's Mistake
The Testing of Tertius
The Japanese: People of the Three Treasures
Night Spell
The Case of the Baker Street Irregular
The Case of the Vanishing Corpse
The Case of the Somerville Secret
The Case of the Threatened King
The Case of the Etruscan Treasure
The Case of the Frightened Friend
The Case of the Murdered Players

The Case
of the Murdered
Players

by Robert Newman

Atheneum 1985 *New York*

Library of Congress in Publication Data

Newman, Robert
The case of the murdered players.

SUMMARY: When two actresses of the London stage
in the 1890s die under circumstances suspiciously
like those that killed three actresses ten years before,
Andrew and Inspector Peter Wyatt fear for
Andrew's actress mother.
1. Children's stories, American. [1. Mystery and
detective stories] I. Title.
PZ7.N4857Casdm 1985   [Fic]   85-7956
ISBN 0-689-31155-9

Contents

The Case
of the Murdered
Players

FOR JEAN KARL—
with admiration,
appreciation and
affection.

1

The Telegram

Standing outside the door, Andrew made a last attempt to guess why the headmaster had sent for him. A summons from that most august person was a startling and anxious-making event at any time. And it was particularly surprising coming now, on the last day of school, just as they were about to go home for the Christmas holidays.

It wasn't his work. As far as he knew, he had done quite well this term, even with the Latin that had given him a certain amount of trouble before this. The fight he had had with Rossiter because of the way he'd bullied the younger boys in the house? Unlikely. The headmaster never interfered in matters of that sort, and besides, that had taken place weeks ago.

Giving up, Andrew knocked at the heavy oak door

and was invited to come in. The headmaster, in his familiar, worn gown, was at his desk.

"Ah, Andrew," he said, looking at him over the top of his spectacles. "I hope my sending for you didn't worry you."

"No, sir. Though it did puzzle me."

"You must have that most estimable of attributes then, a clear conscience. The fact is, a telegram came for you a short while ago." Then, as Andrew looked at him, "I like our boys to read any telegram they may get here in my study. Then, if there's bad news or a problem—if they need advice, help or comfort—I'm here to give it to them."

"I understand, sir."

The headmaster handed him a yellow envelope, and with some anxiety, Andrew tore it open.

"Imperative I see you soon as possible," it read. "Meet me lunch noon tomorrow White Stag. Bring Sara, but tell no one else about this. Repeat, tell no one else!" It was signed Wyatt.

In one sense, the literal one, Andrew had no difficulty understanding this. Wyatt was his friend, Inspector Peter Wyatt of the London Metropolitan Police. The White Stag was a chophouse near Scotland Yard where Andrew had had lunch with Wyatt several times. And Sara was Sara Wiggins, daughter of his mother's housekeeper and an even closer friend than Wyatt. But, in another sense, Andrew did not understand it at all. Why was it urgent that Wyatt see him so quickly? And when he said, 'Tell no one else about this,' did he mean that Andrew was not to tell his mother? Apparently he did. And if so, the question was: Why?

When Andrew raised his eyes, the headmaster was looking at him intently, seriously.

"I hope there's nothing wrong at home, Andrew," he said. "Is there?"

"No, sir. There's nothing wrong. At least . . . No, nothing."

It was a little after five when Andrew got to London. Since he had not been sure what train he would be taking, Fred, the Tillett coachman, was not waiting for him, and he took a four-wheeler from Paddington to the house in St. John's Wood.

Matson, the butler, let him in, and Andrew had barely taken off his coat and hat before Mrs. Wiggins and Sara appeared. Mrs. Wiggins greeted him, as she always did, with an enthusiastic hug and wanted to know if he'd had tea. When he said he had, she went off to the kitchen to make sure that the cook knew he had arrived and that all was going as it should there.

"Is my mother home?" asked Andrew, noticing that Sara was wearing a new dress and looking prettier than ever.

"In her room writing a letter," said Sara, her clipped

and off-handed manner covering the shyness they both always felt when they hadn't seen one another for some time.

"In that case, here. You'd better read this," he said, giving her Wyatt's telegram.

She read it and was looking at him with a puzzled frown that told him she didn't know what it was about either when a door upstairs opened and Verna came hurrying down the stairs.

"Andrew, darling," she said, embracing him. "I thought I heard a cab, but I was in the middle of something and I wasn't sure. How are you?" she asked, holding him away from her and studying him.

"Fine."

"I must say you look well. And of course you've grown again—which I know I'm not supposed to say. And I'm sure Mrs. Wiggins has asked you if you've had tea."

"She has. And I told her I had it on the train, and she's gone into the kitchen to chivvy Mrs. Simmonds who's not going to like it one bit. So let's go inside and sit down so you can tell me how you are."

"Why, I'm fine too," said Verna, leading the way into the parlor.

"No, you're not. What's wrong?"

About to sit down, Verna looked at Sara to see if she'd said anything to him and Sara shook her head.

"What makes you think something's wrong?" she asked.

"I just do. You're angry or upset about something."

"I must say that playing detective with Sara and Peter Wyatt has made you very observant. Or have you become psychic, able to read minds and that sort of thing?"

"No. I just know you. Now what is it?"

Sighing, Verna sat down.

"It's the play."

No need to ask which one. Her last play, an adaptation of *Jane Eyre*, had closed a few weeks before. But long before that, Lawrence Harrison, the manager who was also her good friend, had come to her with a new comedy about which she had been quite excited.

"I thought you liked it."

"I did and do like it. It's not just funny, it's witty. Lydia is just the kind of character I've been dying to play, especially after Jane Eyre. That's why I'm annoyed at Harrison for postponing it."

"Why is he postponing it?"

"That's just it. I don't know. We were supposed to start rehearsals last Wednesday, but I got a note from him saying he was holding off until he had talked to Duncan about some rewriting. It's true that there are some things that can be improved, but nothing serious enough to delay going into rehearsal. There's something very odd about the whole thing, and I don't like it."

"What are you going to do about it?"

"I'm having lunch with Harrison tomorrow, and I'm going to get to the bottom of it."

Andrew and Sara exchanged glances. That took care of that very nicely. If Verna was having lunch with Harrison, there would be no awkward questions asked when they went off to have lunch with Peter Wyatt.

2

The Murdered Players

The White Stag was not yet crowded when Sara and Andrew arrived, and they were able to get the table in the bay window that Andrew knew Wyatt liked. The waiter remembered Andrew and nodded when he said they were waiting for someone. By ten minutes after twelve, Wyatt had still not appeared, and Sara and Andrew were beginning to wonder what had happened, when Sergeant Tucker, the large and deceptively mild-looking policeman who had been working with Wyatt for some time, entered, looked around and came over to them.

"Well," he said. "The troublesome two."

"Troublesome to whom?" asked Andrew.

"Us at the Yard. Though I'll admit you've given a certain amount of trouble to a few yobbos, too."

"I should say we have," said Sara. "You wouldn't

have solved half the cases you have if it wasn't for us. Where's Wyatt?"

"He'll be along. He was on his way here when the commissioner sent for him. So he sent me over to tell you why he was late and that he'd be here when he could."

"Something up?" asked Andrew.

"There's always something up at the Yard. What do you think we do all day, sit around figuring form for the races?"

"I know you do that most of the time. But I meant something important. There must be if the commissioner sent for Wyatt."

"How do you know he didn't want to ask him who his tailor is?"

"He probably asked him that a long time ago," said Sara. "Come on, Sergeant. Tell us."

"I will not. That's how the trouble always starts. Someone tells you three words about a case, and the next thing we know you're in it up to your sit-me-downs."

"All right," said Andrew. "Just tell us if it's animal, vegetable or mineral."

"I'll tell you nothing. I'll tell Frank here," he said to the waiter who had reappeared, "what his nibs is having for lunch. And by the time it gets here, *he'll* be here. A steak and kidney pie for the inspector, Frank."

"And a pint of your best bitter, of course."

"Of course."

Sara and Andrew decided to have steak and kidney pie, too, and Tucker proved to be as good a prophet in this as he was in most things, for about the time the waiter reappeared with their order, Wyatt came hurrying in.

"Sorry I'm late. You explained?" he asked Tucker.

"I did."

"I left a note on your desk. Take care of it as soon as you can."

"Aren't you having lunch with us?" Sara asked Tucker.

"Someone has to hold the fort," said the sergeant. "I'll grab a bite at the pub, but I suspect I'll be seeing the two of you again sometime soon." And giving them an exaggerated salute, he left.

"How's the commissioner?" asked Sara.

"Fine."

"Do you think you'll be able to take care of what he wanted to see you about?" asked Andrew.

"As always, I intend to do my best."

"All right," said Sara. "We give up. So you don't intend to tell us what the commissioner wanted or about the case you're on. What did you want to see us about?"

"It's the holiday season. Andrew has just come back to London after several months away at school, and I haven't seen you since he was last here. Isn't that enough reason to want to see the two of you?"

"To send me a telegram making an appointment for my first day home?" said Andrew. "The answer is no."

"Why do you think I wanted to see you?"

"I don't mind guessing when it serves some useful purpose. But since you're bound to tell us sooner or later, I'll just wait until you do."

"You get more difficult every time I see you," said Wyatt.

"You say that every time we see *you*," said Sara. "And then you give us that look."

"What look is that?"

"The one that asks, 'Can I trust them to do what I want and keep quiet about it?' And the ridiculous part of it is that you must have decided that you *could* trust us or you never would have sent Andrew that telegram."

"True. All right, I'll tell you. Do you read the newspapers when you're away at school, Andrew?"

"No, I don't."

"Even though you're here, I don't imagine you do either, Sara."

"No. If something happens that Miss Tillett thinks I'll be interested in, she tells me about it or shows it to me. But that's all. Why? Has anything happened that we should know about?"

"Yes. Two weeks ago an actress, not too well known here in London but quite well known in the provinces, was found dead in her dressing room in the Adelphi Theatre. About a week ago another actress—I call her that though her most recent engagement was working with a magician at the Vaudeville Theatre—was found dead in the alley outside the stage door of the theatre. Both deaths were reported in the papers. But another one was not. That took place the day before yesterday. The victim was Meg Morrissey, who had a fairly important part in the musical, *The Girl From Fiji*, at the Garrick. Any comments or questions?"

"Questions," said Andrew. "You say these actresses were found dead. Were they murdered?"

"Yes."

"How?"

"At the moment, that's not important. There are other, more important things to discuss."

"They were all actresses, and they were all playing in theatres around the same area," said Sara. "Around the Strand."

"Right."

"You said that the first two deaths were reported in the newspapers, but the last one wasn't," said Andrew. "How did that happen?"

"I've been handling the cases, and I was able to keep the last one quiet."

"That's what I thought. Why did you do it? I mean, why was it important to keep it quiet?"

"To understand that, I'll have to give you some history." Wyatt cut a neat portion of steak and kidney pie, ate it and washed it down with a draught of beer. "Almost exactly ten years ago, at the beginning of the Christmas season, there was another series of strange deaths, all connected with the theatre. Four of them in all."

"When you say strange deaths, do you mean that they were all murders, too?" asked Andrew.

"They were never called murders," said Wyatt. "In fact, in three of the cases no one was sure what the cause of death was. But I'm convinced now that they *were* murders. In the fourth case, the man died of a heart attack as a result of the deaths."

"And the reason you kept the last murder quiet," said Sara, "is that you don't want people to start remembering those earlier deaths and start thinking there may be more of them."

"Exactly. We don't see any reason to frighten people unnecessarily."

"Because, of course, when they do get frightened," said Sara, "they have a way of going after the police, wanting to know why they're not doing something about it when you're already doing everything you can."

"How well you understand us," said Wyatt dryly.

"What I don't understand is why you're telling us about it," said Andrew. "I mean, it's not as if—" He broke off. "My mother!"

"Yes, Andrew."

"Is she in any danger?"

"We don't know, because we don't know what's behind these latest killings, what the motive is. All we know is that they all involved actresses."

"But she's not actually in a play right now," said Sara. "At least . . . Was *that* your doing too, getting Mr. Harrison to postpone rehearsals of the play?"

"Yes. I told him why, but I didn't tell her. I didn't see any point in alarming her. But I thought I'd tell the two of you so that, if it's necessary, you could help persuade her to stay off the stage for a while."

"Of course," said Andrew. "Though I think you'd be better off telling her the truth than pretending there's something wrong with the play as Mr. Harrison's been doing. In fact . . . What is it?" he asked as Wyatt sat up, staring past him.

"The chap who just came in," said Wyatt.

Turning, Andrew saw a sullen-looking man in rather flashy clothes who stood just inside the restaurant door.

"What about him?"

"His name's Bolan, Nifty Bolan, and he's a well-known cracksman. Do you know what that is?"

"A burglar who specializes in opening safes," said Sara.

"Right. He's been in jail for over three years now, and I assume he's just been released. But what is he doing here in the Yard's backyard?" He smiled faintly as Sergeant Tucker came back into the restaurant and stood behind Bolan, looking from him to Wyatt. "Tucker must have seen him go by, and he's wondering about it too, wants to make sure I know he's here."

He nodded to Tucker, and the sergeant left. Immediately after the door closed, it was pushed open again and an interesting-looking man came in. He was in his late thirties or early forties, not quite as tall as Bolan, but sturdy and with a pleasant, open face. He was wearing a tweed overcoat and a soft felt hat, and he looked like a country squire in town for the day. He greeted Bolan and started to lead him to a table that Frank, the waiter, had evidently been saving for him. Then, seeing Wyatt, he paused, said something to Bolan and came over to the table.

"This is a pleasant surprise, Inspector."

"It shouldn't be too big a surprise. I frequently have lunch here. I'd like you to meet two young friends of mine, Sara Wiggins and Andrew Tillett. Nicholas Norwood."

"Nice to meet you," said Norwood, bowing politely. Then, to Wyatt, "I'd like *you* to meet the man I'm lunching with. In fact, I was planning to come over to the Yard later on and see if you could spare us a few minutes."

"Is the man you want me to meet Nifty Bolan?"

"Why, yes. Do you know him?"

"By name, sight and reputation. But since we're well along with our lunch, why don't you bring him over here when you've finished yours?"

"Your young friends won't mind?"

"My young friends have another appointment and have to leave very soon."

"In that case, splendid. We'll be along shortly." And bowing again to Sara and Andrew, he left to join Bolan at a table on the far side of the restaurant.

"What made you say we had another appointment?" asked Sara.

"I just thought it might be better if you did have. I doubt if either Norwood or Bolan would talk as freely in front of you as they will to me alone."

"That's what I thought," said Andrew. "Who is Norwood?"

"Quite an interesting man. Did you ever hear of the Golden Rule Society?"

"No."

"Well, he started it, runs it. Do you know what the Golden Rule is?"

"From the Bible, isn't it?"

"Matthew. 'Do unto others as you would have them do unto you.'"

"What does it do?" asked Andrew. "The society. I mean."

"Works with old lags, criminals who have been released from prison. Helps them and their families by lending them money and helping them get legitimate jobs."

"Good show!" said Sara. "What made Mr. Norwood do it?"

"That's what I asked him the first time I met him," said Wyatt. "It seems he comes of an old county family with an estate near Stanbury. His father was one of those hunting, fishing squires who wasn't the least bit interested in his children, and Norwood's best friend when he was growing up was a man who worked on the estate and taught young Norwood a great deal about animals, birds and fish. When Norwood went away to school, the man was caught poaching by the Norwood gamekeeper. They fought, he broke the gamekeeper's arm and was sent to jail. When he was released, he couldn't get work, and he had a family to take care of, so he started poaching again. He was sent to jail again, and this time he got jail fever and died there."

"But that's awful!" said Andrew.

"That's what Norwood thought," said Wyatt. "He

was away at Oxford at the time, didn't know anything about it until it was too late. When he found out about it, he had a terrible fight with his father, wouldn't talk to him for several years. Then, when his father died and he inherited the estate, he started the Golden Rule Society to try to keep the same thing from happening again."

"Good for him!" said Sara.

"I agree," said Wyatt. "It's something the government should be doing. No matter what it cost, in the long run it would save not only lives, but money—which is one of the few things the state seems to understand. You'll forgive me for sending you off, then?"

"Of course," said Andrew. "As for the other thing we talked about, as I said, I think you should tell my mother the truth instead of having Mr. Harrison pretend there's something wrong with the play. But, whatever you do, of course I'll back you up, make sure she doesn't appear on stage anywhere until you're convinced she won't be in danger."

"All right, Andrew. You may be right about the direct approach. Your mother's not an easy person to fool. I'll think about it. And I'm sure I'll be seeing the two of you again soon."

The two young people left, and Wyatt ordered another pint of bitter and some Stilton cheese. He was just finishing both when Norwood appeared at the table with Bolan.

"May we join you now?" he asked.

"Please do. Can I offer you some bitter or cheese?"

"Thank you, no. Bolan says that he knows a good deal about you, as you do about him, even though you've never met."

"Well, now that we've remedied that, why don't the two of you sit down?"

"Thanks, guv'nor," said Bolan.

"What are you up to these days, Nifty?" asked Wyatt.

"That's one of the things we've been talking about," said Norwood. "Bolan thought that he'd like to work with a locksmith or a safe manufacturer. He knows a great deal about both, but I told him I didn't think that was a good idea."

"I agree. I think his interest in safes and locks might be misunderstood."

"Exactly. But I was able to get him a job in a machine shop in Southwark, and he and his new employer seem happy about it. But that's not what we wanted to talk to you about. Tell him, Bolan."

"All right. Do you remember old Harry Hopwood, Inspector?"

"Of course. He was one of the first major arrests I made."

"Right. Nabbed him after that break-in on Greek Street you did. But there was a good deal of swag that was never recovered. Lot of old coins, for instance."

"Yes. There was a goodish reward offered for their return."

"Right. Well, old Harry's dead, died about two months ago. We was pals in the clink, and knowing he was mortal sick and not likely to make it out the gate, he told me where he'd hid the stuff, and I thought I'd like to tell you."

"Oh? To collect the reward?"

"No. I don't want the reward. They can give it to Mr. Norwood here for that society of his. I'm just trying to prove to everyone that, from now on, I'm really going straight."

"Nifty, I won't say I'm surprised," said Wyatt, "because I'm not. I'm dumbfounded, dumb-foozled and just plain bowled over!"

3

A Startling Revelation

It was getting dark when Sara and Andrew got off the bus and walked home up Rysdale Road. Just before they reached the house, they met the lamplighter, an elderly man with a grey mustache, who nodded to them and smiled. Remembering his first evening in London—the first time he had seen a lamplighter—Andrew paused and watched as he pushed his long pole up under the glass shade of the gaslight, turned on the gas and lit it, then went on, the yellow glow high up on the iron standards marking his progress.

When they left The White Stag, Sara and Andrew had walked over to the Drury Lane Theatre near Covent Garden, where Andrew had bought tickets for the pantomime the next afternoon. Sara had protested rather feebly, not sure that Andrew really wanted to

go and reluctant to have him spend the money, especially for good seats in the stalls, if he didn't. But
he had paid no attention to her, assuring her that he
was as anxious to see the pantomime as she was. That,
in fact, it wouldn't seem like the Christmas season if
he didn't go.

From the Drury Lane they walked over to Liberty's, an architectural jumble of a store with balconies
and enclosed courtyards strewn with all the colors
and fabrics of the Arabian Nights; and there Sara
helped Andrew pick out a shawl as a Christmas present
for his mother, a cashmere with a muted paisley pat-
tern. And as the shawl was being wrapped, he saw
Sara looking at a silk scarf and was thus able to determine, as he had hoped he would, what he should get
her for Christmas.

Verna was already home when they got there, and
Andrew barely had time to give his package to Matson and ask him to hide it before Verna came downstairs looking like a stormcloud sweeping down from
the Alps. No, they told her, they hadn't had tea and
followed her into the sitting room while Matson went
to inform the cook that they were home.

"You don't look as if you had a very good lunch,"
said Andrew.

"There was nothing wrong with the lunch, but
there certainly is something wrong with Harrison,"
said Verna. "I don't know what's come over him. Up

to now I trusted him so completely that I kept saying I didn't know why we bothered with contracts. That his word was good enough for me. But today I didn't believe anything he said."

"You're talking about the reasons he gave you for postponing the play?"

"Yes."

"What did he say?" asked Sara.

"The same thing he said before. That the play needed more work. Well, I know that. I was the one who first said the second act could use another scene. But we agreed that it was a small thing and we should go into rehearsal while Duncan did something about it. But now Harrison says he doesn't want to commit himself until he sees what Duncan does. Yes, Matson?" she said as the butler knocked discreetly at the door.

"Inspector Wyatt is here and would like to see you."

"Show him in. And ask Annie to bring in another cup. I'm sure he'd like some tea also."

Matson bowed and left.

"Good evening, Peter," said Verna when Wyatt came in. "I won't ask you how you are because it's obvious you're in a temper."

Wyatt would have been hard put to deny it, for if Verna looked like a stormcloud, he looked like a typhoon.

"I take it you haven't seen this afternoon's *Journal*," he said.

"I never see it," said Verna. "It's a loathesome sheet."

"It is. But since someone is bound to show you a copy of today's, I thought it had better be me." And taking a folded copy of the newspaper from his pocket, he gave it to her, pointing to an article marked with red ink.

"Meg Morrissey dead!" she said after she'd read a few lines. "Murdered! I knew her! Not well, but I did know her. And I liked her!"

"I thought you knew her," said Wyatt. "That's why I was sure that someone would show you the article. It's a story written by a reporter named Fulton," he said to Sara and Andrew. "And he's covered, not only this murder and the other two I told you about at lunch, but the ones that took place ten years ago."

"What's that?" said Verna, looking up from the newspaper. "You had lunch together, you and Andrew?"

"And Sara. Yes."

"Did you meet specifically to talk about these murders—Meg Morrissey's and the others he mentions?"

"We did."

"But why?"

"Did you finish the article?"

"You mean where he talks about the fact that this may just be the beginning? That . . . Wait a minute. Are you suggesting that *I* might be in danger?"

"Isn't that what *he* suggests—though he's careful not to mention you or anyone else by name?"

"Yes, but he's just a Fleet Street faker, the worst kind of yellow journalist. Do you mean you think so too?"

"I do."

"Well," she said, and her voice was cold and cutting, "this is getting more and more interesting. You admit that you met with Andrew and Sara to discuss these deaths, the very farfetched possibility that I might be threatened. Did you, by any chance, discuss this with anyone else?"

"If you mean Mr. Harrison, the answer is yes."

"I knew it! Knew there was something wrong there —that Harrison wasn't telling me the truth. But it never occurred to me that it would be anything like this! That someone I had considered a friend would go behind my back, connive with my son and my manager . . ."

"Connive?"

"Isn't that what you were doing?"

"No!"

"I don't think you're being fair, Mother," said Andrew.

There was something wrong here, something he did not understand. Because, from the time they had first met, Verna and Wyatt had seemed to admire one another greatly. But now here they were sparring with one another like a pair of hereditary enemies.

"What do you call it if not conniving?" said Verna. "If you felt that there was reason to be anxious about my safety—grounds real enough to warrant my keeping off the stage for a while—why didn't you come to me openly and tell me about it?"

"Because I was afraid that you would do exactly what you're doing—respond, not rationally, but emotionally!"

"When you say emotionally, what you really mean is hysterically, don't you?"

"If I meant hysterically," said Wyatt, his voice rising slightly as Verna's had become colder, "I would say hysterically!"

"I don't know if I believe that. In fact, I'm not sure I believe anything you say! It seems to me that things must be very slow over at Scotland Yard for you to get this exercised over something as ridiculous as this!"

"Mother, please . . ." said Andrew.

"May I point out to you, Miss Tillett, that what we're talking about—what you're calling ridiculous— is a possible threat to your life?"

"And why is that of such cardinal importance to you?"

"Because I'm a policeman. Because it's my job to prevent crimes as well as capture those who commit them. And because the most heinous, the most abhorrent of all crimes are the ones in which someone's life is threatened. Does that answer your question?"

"Not entirely."

"I didn't think it would. All right." His voice dropped in register but became more intense. "While it would be my job to worry about anyone in the circumstances we've been discussing, no matter how difficult you've been—and you've been very difficult indeed—I worry more about you than I would about anyone else because . . ." He hesitated.

"Yes?"

"Because I love you, dammit! I have from the first time I met you, and if you hadn't become so completely impossible, I'd ask you to marry me!"

"Oh," said Verna quietly, even demurely, and without the slightest bit of surprise. "Well, of course, that's different."

"What did you say?"

"I said, that's different."

Andrew jumped as Sara kicked him in the ankle. Closing his mouth, which had opened in astonishment, he looked at her. She got up, pulled him to his feet and led him from the room. It was only when they were outside and the door had closed behind them that the full significance of what had just happened dawned on him. That and something else. The fact that though he had been astonished, Sara had been as little surprised at what had been said as Verna.

4

The Old Deaths and the New

"Well," said Sara, sitting down on the bench that was just outside the parlor door. "How do you feel about it?"

"About what?"

"About what just happened."

"Why, I don't know. After all, it doesn't have anything to do with me."

But even as he said that, he realized that wasn't true. It had a great deal to do with him. If matters followed their usual course, and Verna married Wyatt —and remembering things that he had paid little attention to at the time, he was suddenly convinced that she would marry him—then Wyatt would become his stepfather.

"I'll admit I've been pretty dim, but I never did think of the two of them that way. I take it you did."

"Yes."

"Well, it's strange. I never knew my father. He died before I was born. And so, while it's taken me by surprise, I think I'd like it. I mean, why shouldn't I like it when I like him—Peter—so much?"

"Liking him—and I know you do like him—and liking the idea of having him marry your mother are two very different things. Not that you're going to have too much to say about it."

"I don't think I will either. Is she going to say yes to him?"

"Of course."

"I think so, too. Well, there's no point in our waiting out here. I don't imagine we'll be seeing either of them for some time."

"I think we will," said Sara confidently.

"Why?"

"Because your mother's a very intelligent, sensitive woman."

As she said this, the door opened, and Wyatt looked out.

"Oh, there you are. We hoped you hadn't really sloped off. Do you want to come back inside?"

"Do you want us to?" asked Andrew.

"Of course we do," said Verna. She looked intently at Andrew as he came back into the room. "It was very discreet of you to leave when you did, darling, but it wasn't really necessary."

"Actually, it wasn't my idea. It was Sara's. I was too surprised to think of going. Or of anything else."

"I know. It did come as rather a surprise. But now that you've had a chance to think about it, how do you feel about it?"

"That's what Sara asked me just a minute ago, and ...I'm glad, Mother. I'm very glad."

"Oh," said Verna, coloring with pleasure. "I'm happy that you're glad. Because, while I haven't said anything definite yet, I'm more inclined to say yes to Peter's odd and abrupt proposal than anything else."

"Odd and abrupt?" said Wyatt. "The whole thing was a tricksy diddle, a form of entrapment on your part. Because, as I'm sure you know, a proposal of marriage was the last thing I had on my mind when I came here. I came because of that piece in the paper, because I was concerned about your safety, and—"

"Well, since, as I said, I haven't given you a definite answer yet, there's no need for you to feel committed. In fact—"

"Since that particular discussion concerns only you and Peter," said Andrew, "and I suspect it will go on for some time, may I suggest that you postpone it for the time being and we go back to what began all this, the matter of your safety?"

"I would have thought," said Verna, "that my possible marriage would have been of just as much interest to you as an extremely hypothetical danger. However . . ."

"Thank you, Andrew," said Wyatt. "I'm very anxious to get back to the matter of the mysterious deaths because, when we stopped discussing them, your mother was still resisting the idea of staying off the stage until we had the matter in hand."

"I still think it's nonsense," said Verna. "But I'm willing to listen to anything you have to say about it."

"Well, that's progress," said Wyatt. "Very well. Let's begin with the deaths that took place ten years ago. I don't imagine you remember them."

"But I do," said Verna. "I was just beginning to get parts then and I'd been to see Ben Wallace several times —he was a very well-known manager—and I admired Nina Wallace enormously. But I don't know what was so mysterious about their deaths. I mean, I know there was some uncertainty as to how Nina had died, but I don't think there was any about Ben Wallace. He was mad about her, and almost immediately after she died, he had a heart attack."

"Quite true," said Wyatt. "I spent a good deal of time looking into the matter, and his death was the only one that was definitely and satisfactorily explained medically."

"Who were the others?" asked Sara. "And what happened to them?"

"They were both actresses, too. One of them, Aggie Russell, was a friend of Nina's and had been to see her shortly before she died. She died herself the next day, and so did another actress, May Mallory, who didn't seem to have any direct connection with them. As to how they died, when you read the reports you realize that doctors can do just as much waffling as the police when they don't know the answer to something. They talk of seizures and strokes, but they don't come out flatly and say that's what they died of."

"Am I right in suspecting you don't think they died of natural causes?" said Verna.

"Yes."

"Why?"

"Because I feel there's a connection of some sort between those deaths and the ones that have just taken place. And though we've said nothing about it to the press, we know that the most recent ones were murders."

"Committed how?" asked Andrew.

Wyatt hesitated. "I don't like to talk about it because it's very strange and very frightening. They were stabbed."

"Stabbed?"

"Yes, but in a very odd way. Did you ever hear of pithing?"

They shook their heads.

"It's a technique doctors and scientists use to kill

33

laboratory animals painlessly and instantaneously. It's done by destroying the spinal cord or the brain with a needle."

Verna shuddered and lost her color.

"Are you saying that that's how Meg Morrissey was killed?"

"Yes. She and the other two actresses."

"And you think that the ones who died ten years ago were killed in the same way?" asked Sara.

"I think it's possible. The weapon, a needle not much larger than a sailmaker's needle, did not leave a wound that was obvious or easy to detect. It just so happened that the doctor who performed the recent autopsy is extremely good. He discovered the wounds and was able to tell us the cause of death. He also told us that there have been great strides made recently in forensic medicine—medicine used to detect crimes— and said that it was quite possible that similar wounds could have been overlooked by doctors ten years ago."

"Am I right in thinking that not just anyone could have committed the murders?" asked Andrew. "I mean, it's not like an ordinary knifing. Whoever did them must have been very skillful, known a good deal about medicine."

"So it would seem."

"And you've no idea who could have committed the murders or why?" asked Verna.

"Let's say I have the beginning of an idea—a possible hypothesis."

"Tell us."

"All right. As I said, I've been doing some investigating and I found someone who told me some interesting things. Her name is Emmie Madden, and she was Nina Wallace's dresser. She's retired, but I was able to trace her to where she's living with her daughter in Bethnal Green."

"How old is she?" asked Verna.

"Oh, late sixties. But very alert, and her memory seemed very good. I told her why I was interested in Nina Wallace's death—and before I could even get to any questions she said she'd always felt that there was something very strange about it."

"Did she say why?" asked Sara.

"No, and I suspect it was just a way of indicating that she was upset. But when I asked her if there was anyone in the company who might have some reason for wanting to see Nina Wallace dead, she gave me an odd look and said, 'That's a rum one, your asking that. Because there was someone around I always felt a bit funny about.' Her name," he said looking at Verna, "was apparently Sally Siddons."

"No, I don't know her," said Verna. "Not that that means anything. Any relation to Sarah Siddons?"

"I don't think so. I'm quite sure it wasn't her real

name. But it's significant that she named herself for one of our greatest actresses."

"What did she do, this Sally Siddons?" asked Sara.

"Not very much," said Wyatt. "She was quite pretty according to Emmie Madden, but not much of an actress. She played bit parts in Wallace's pantomimes, but she did have aspirations, and as a result, she became involved with Ben Wallace himself."

"Involved how?" asked Andrew.

"The way a girl can become involved with a man when his wife is away. Because Nina Wallace was out of town for most of the summer. Well, Sally came around one day, and it was clear that she was going to have a baby and Emmie Madden had a feeling that Ben Wallace was the father—a suspicion that was fairly well confirmed when Sally hinted that *she* was going to play the lead in the Christmas pantomime, not Nina Wallace."

"And did she?" asked Verna.

"No, she didn't. But Nina Wallace didn't either. Because shortly after the pantomime went into rehearsal, Nina Wallace died. Ben Wallace was on the continent at the time, and when he came back and learned what had happened, he died too—of a heart attack."

"I think I know what you're suggesting," said Andrew. "But I'm not really sure."

"I said it was only a hypothesis, but suppose that

when young Sally discovered that she was going to have a baby, she went to Wallace and told him about it and also told him that she wanted to play the lead in the Christmas pantomime. He would have been shocked at that. He would probably have been glad to pay for the support of the child and help her get a job. But he couldn't possibly give her the lead in the panto because that was the part his wife played. And even if Sally were as good as Nina—which of course she wasn't—he wasn't going to jeopardize his marriage by giving the part to her instead of his wife. Well, suppose Sally listened to him and said to herself in her naive way—for I gather she was a little simple —'He won't give me the part because of his wife. But suppose something happened to his wife? I'll bet he'd give it to me then.' "

"Are you saying that she killed Nina Wallace in order to get the part?" asked Sara in a hushed voice.

"I said it was a supposition. I was wondering if it wasn't possible."

"Have you any facts at all to back up your supposition?" asked Verna.

"There is something. I don't know if you can call it a fact, but . . . As I said, Ben Wallace was on the continent when his wife died. He came back terribly shaken. Emmie Madden remembers how broken up he was, because apparently he did love his wife very much. Then, two days later, he died of a heart attack.

Now if his heart attack was related to his wife's death, what could he have discovered that was even more of a shock to him than the fact of her death?"

"The realization of how and why she had died," said Verna after a pause. "If Sally Siddons either told him—or said something that led him to guess—that she had killed his wife."

"Exactly. I think the knowledge that he had been at least partly responsible for his wife's death because of his involvement with Sally Siddons would have been enough to kill him."

Again they were silent for a moment, as if trying to digest this.

"All right," said Andrew finally. "Suppose you're right about that murder. What about the other ones? Did Sally Siddons commit them, too?"

"I think it's possible," said Wyatt. "According to the notes on the case, Agnes Russell, the second actress who was found dead, was a friend of Nina Wallace's and had been to see her earlier in the evening on the night that she was found dead."

"You think that she might have seen Sally Siddons or whoever killed Nina Wallace, or knew that she was going to be coming there, and that she was killed to keep her from saying anything about it," said Sara.

"Yes."

"What about the third murder?" asked Andrew.

"I could find no logical connection between it and

the other two. One thought occurred to me—a motive that would make it the most cold-blooded killing of all. That was that the murder was committed precisely *because* it had no connection with the others, a kind of red herring to draw attention away from the fact that the other two *were* connected."

"You're right," said Andrew. "That is horrible, really horrible. But say that everything you've said is true, what possible connection can those murders that were committed ten years ago have with the ones that have just been committed now?"

"I don't know. I just know that I'm very worried. Can't you see how I would be?" he said to Verna. "It's a very frightening situation at best. And when I think that you—you of all people—might be in danger . . ."

"I understand, Peter," said Verna with unaccustomed meekness. "And I promise to be good. To keep off the stage until you discover who's responsible for these horrible deaths and tell me it's safe to go back on the boards again."

5

Ill Met on Regent Street

Sara and Andrew were quiet as they got off a dark green City Atlas omnibus at Oxford Circus and walked down Regent Street. They had done very little talking since the startling events of the previous afternoon. They had avoided discussing the mysterious deaths; the subject was too frightening. The only aspect of it in which they took any comfort was the fact that Verna had agreed to stay off the stage until the murderer had been caught and Wyatt was sure that she would not be in any danger if she appeared.

They were on their way now to meet Verna and Wyatt for, learning that they were going to the pantomime, Wyatt announced that he and Verna had something to do on Regent Street and suggested that they meet there and have lunch together.

They walked slowly, partly because they were early and partly because Regent Street was more crowded now, during this period before Christmas, than any other time of the year. This was not a street of large and important stores like Liberty's, Swan and Edgar and Peter Robinson, but rather was where you found very special shops; Hamley's, for instance, greatest of all toy stores, Negretti and Zambra, purveyors of optical equipment, whose name sounded like an incantation, and of course many jewelers and silversmiths.

They paused in front of Worthington's, the old and established jeweler that was their objective.

"There they are," said Sara.

"Where?" said Andrew, looking past the candlesticks and the elaborate silver tea sets in the window. Then, seeing his mother and Wyatt at a counter being waited on solicitously by a clerk in a frock coat, "Oh, yes. I see them. Shall we go in?"

"No," said Sara, a little awkwardly. "Let's wait."

"Why? We *were* early, but we're not now. We're right on time."

"I still think we should wait."

"And I asked you why."

"What do you think they're doing?"

"I don't know. Buying something, I suppose."

"But what?"

"I don't know." He looked through the window again. Verna and Wyatt were bent over a tray, examining its contents. Then, as Verna picked something up, slipped it on her finger . . . "A ring?"

"Yes. What kind?"

"I suppose . . . an engagement ring."

"Exactly. And I think they should be left alone, given a chance to select one by themselves."

"Oh. Yes," said Andrew, looking at her with respect. "I think you're right. Shall we wait here or shall we go look in some other shop window?"

"No reason why we can't wait here as long as we don't go in."

"All right," said Andrew. Then, looking at a pair of magnificent, life-sized silver pheasants that were in the center of the window, "What do you suppose those are for?"

"Table decorations."

"Probably. And what about these?" he asked, moving over to a pair of epergnes that flanked an elaborate, decorated silver bowl.

"I think they're to hold fruit."

"How do you know so much about these things?"

"I read about them in magazines. And while your mother doesn't often give formal dinner parties, the parents of some of the girls at school do, and I've seen the tables being set."

A man who had been walking up Regent Street glanced at them as he went by, hesitated, and then came back.

"Miss Wiggins?" he said, raising a rather battered bowler politely.

"Yes," said Sara.

"I'm Edward Fulton of the *Journal*. You probably don't remember me, but I met you, talked to you, when you were playing in *Jane Eyre*."

"Yes, of course I remember. You came to interview Miss Tillett, but I was in her dressing room at the time, and she suggested that you talk to me also."

"That's right. And it made a very interesting piece —young actress, just beginning her career."

His face was thin and his eyes were sharp, and they kept moving constantly, looking from Sara to Andrew and then back again.

"I've no idea whether I have a career in the theatre or not," said Sara. "I got the part mostly because I knew Miss Tillett; but now I'm back at school again and I'm not sure I'll even be in another play."

"Of course you will. I thought you were very good, very talented," said Fulton. He had looked from them into the shop and now his eyes widened slightly. "Isn't that Inspector Wyatt in there?"

"Yes. We're waiting for him."

"That's right. I'd heard you know him. What's he

doing in Worthington's? Making sure the jewels are safe?"

"The jewels?"

"The Maharajah's jewels. You mean you don't know about them?"

"No."

"I thought you were a friend of his. The Maharajah of Ghazipur came here about a week ago bringing a diamond as large as the Star of India and several other stones that he's going to present to Her Majesty. He turned them over to Worthington's to be polished and set, and he also gave them some of his own jewels. Scotland Yard has tried to keep the whole thing quiet, but the word is that it's probably the largest and most valuable collection of jewels we've ever had in England—outside of the crown jewels in the Tower, of course."

"And you think that the inspector's in there making sure that everything's secure?" said Andrew.

"Of course. Stands to reason that he would, doesn't it? Oh-oh. He's seen me, and I'm afraid I'm not in his good books right now. I'd better scarper. Toodle-oo!" and he hurried off up the street.

"Was that Fulton of the *Journal*?" asked Wyatt, coming out of the shop.

"Yes," said Andrew.

"I thought so. Fulton!" he called. "Hoy! Hold up there! I want to talk to you!" But instead of stopping,

Fulton increased his pace and disappeared into a crowd of shoppers.

"Well, I'll catch up with him one of these days," said Wyatt. "What did he want?"

"We don't know," said Sara. "He saw us and remembered me from *Jane Eyre* and stopped to talk. He said he wasn't in your good books right now, but he didn't say why."

"You know why. It was he who wrote that piece about Meg Morrissey's murder when we'd specifically asked the press to keep quiet about it."

"Oh, Lord, of course," said Andrew. "I thought his name sounded familiar, but I couldn't place it."

"He told us about the Maharajah's jewels," said Sara, "wanted to know if you were in Worthington's to make sure they were safe."

"What did you say?"

"Nothing," said Andrew. "We didn't know about them."

"Did he say anything about your mother?"

"No. I don't think he saw her when he looked in. He just saw you."

"Well, I suppose we should be thankful for small blessings."

"Oh, there you are," said Verna as she was bowed out of Worthington's by the man in the frock coat. "Have you been here long?"

"No, just a few minutes," said Andrew.

"Why didn't you come in?"

Andrew glanced at Sara. "We didn't mind waiting outside," he said.

"I think that what we're faced with," said Wyatt, "is an excess of discretion, which, while unnecessary, does have its charm. But that's enough of that. Let's go to lunch."

He led them to the Burlington, on the corner of New Burlington Street, where he had booked a table to which they were conducted with a good deal of ceremony by the headwaiter, who stood by while they ordered.

"And now," said Wyatt when the headwaiter and the other waiters had gone, "what do you think we were doing in Worthington's?"

"It was Sara's guess that you were buying a ring," said Andrew.

"As usual," said Wyatt, "Sara was right."

"May we see it?" said Sara.

Verna hesitated a moment, then took a box from her purse and opened it, showing them a gold ring set with a small but exquisitely cut diamond.

"It's beautiful!" said Sara. "But why aren't you wearing it?"

"I don't know," said Verna. "I suppose because I feel a little awkward about it. After all, I'm not exactly a young and blushing bride-to-be."

"Because you have a son?" said Wyatt. "That has

nothing to do with it. As for the rest, knowing your talent, I'm sure you could blush if you thought it was necessary. So, as a favor to Sara as well as me, won't you wear it?"

"Since you ask me so nicely, yes," said Verna and, taking off her glove, put the ring on. "It really is lovely, darling," she said, holding it up. "Thank you."

"No," said Wyatt. "Thank *you*." And leaning over, he kissed her lightly on the cheek. "All of which calls for a small celebration, which, with my usual foresight, I have of course provided for."

He signaled to the headwaiter, who brought over a silver ice bucket with a bottle of champagne in it, which he twirled dextrously to chill before opening.

"On an occasion like this," Wyatt went on, "I think the young people should be permitted to join us, don't you, my dear?"

"I certainly do," said Verna, smiling at the two of them.

6

Aladdin's Lamp

Fred took Sara and Andrew to the Drury Lane Theatre. He had been waiting with the brougham in the
Burlington Mews and was happy to have a chance to
warm the horses up a bit before he took Verna to finish
her shopping. Wyatt had teased Sara and Andrew before they left, saying he was astonished that two young
people, old enough to drink champagne, should be interested in anything as childish as pantomime. But
Andrew had countered by quoting his housemaster at
school, who was a great admirer of pantomime, claim-
ing that it was a national institution that was typically
and uniquely British.

"What's typical about it?" Wyatt had asked. "And
what's unique."

It was typically British, Andrew had said, because
it was made up of so many different elements, each

borrowed from a different country. Its name came from Greece by way of Rome, some of its most important characters came from the Italian *commedia del arte* and its plots from Continental folk tales or the Arabian Nights. And it was unique because it mixed together so many different kinds of theatre: drama, opera, ballet, music hall turns and musical comedy. On top of all this, it played fast and loose with genders in that that the juvenile lead—the principal boy— was always played by a woman while the female comic was played by a man.

At this point Wyatt had thrown up his hands and confessed that, though he had not had the benefit of such a scholarly analysis before, he liked pantomime also and wished he could have gone with the two of them.

After arranging to pick them up after the performance, Fred went back to call for Verna, and Sara and Andrew went into the theatre. As was to be expected, there wasn't an empty seat in the house. The play was *Aladdin*, with the lead played by Lily de Lille, a well-known musical comedy star who, like most of the other actors in the production, only played in pantomime during this time of year.

The orchestra began the overture, the curtain went up and Andrew found himself as carried away by the music and the theatrical magic as he had been when he saw his first pantomime several years before.

When Aladdin came on, Andrew had to admit that Miss de Lille made a handsome and convincing boy; slim and elegant and with a lovely voice as she sang the opening song.

Though the pantomime followed the general line of the original story, there were of course constant additions and interruptions. Aladdin's song attracted the attention of the wicked magician, who asked Aladdin if he would help him with something, and the first transformation took place when the curtain came down briefly to rise on the vast, enchanted cave.

Another of the elements for which the pantomime was famous—its theatrical effects—came shortly after that when Aladdin accidentally rubbed the lamp that the magician had sent him into the cave to get and the genie appeared, floating in the air high over his head.

If the first act introduced the transformation and the special effect, the second act demonstrated the lavishness for which the pantomime was also known, with dozens and dozens of extras in colorful costumes and, not only more songs and dancing, but jugglers and tumblers as well.

In the last act the pantomime reached its climax with the marriage of Aladdin and the princess, the theft of the lamp and the kidnapping of the princess by the wicked magician and the conclusion, when Aladdin gets the lamp and the princess back again and imprisons the wicked magician in the cave where the lamp had originally been hidden. Then, in a typical finale, with the whole company on stage, the principals came down to the footlights, singing:

"We've brought our story to an end.
For our success we must on you depend.
May we, dear friends, your kind applause exhort
To bring our vessel safely into port."

Though traditional, this closing appeal was completely unnecessary for, with a houseful of enthusiastic children, the applause that followed was as loud and sustained as Andrew had ever heard in a theatre.

"Would you like to go backstage?" asked Sara as they put on their hats and coats.

"I don't mind," said Andrew. "Is there someone you want to see?"

"The wardrobe mistress was in charge of costumes in *Jane Eyre.* I ran into her the other day, told her we were probably coming to see *Aladdin,* and she made me promise I'd come backstage if we did."

"I think I remember her," said Andrew. "Wasn't she a jolly-looking woman with her hair in a bun on top of her head?"

"That's right. Her name's Nora Abbott, and I'm sure she'll remember you because she loves your mother."

Mrs. Abbott did remember Andrew, was delighted

to see him and Sara, and insisted on introducing them to Lilly de Lille, who knew Verna slightly and was very happy to hear that they had liked the pantomime. Then Mrs. Abbott introduced them to the stage manager, who showed them some of the devices that were behind the special effects, particularly the one known as the star trap, a platform under the stage that allowed a character to make a sudden and mysterious appearance through a trapdoor. Andrew asked if this had been used when the genie made his appearance and was told that he was let down on a cable from above under the cover of a puff of smoke.

With Nora Abbott watching with proprietary pride, the stage manager was showing them how the scrims and curtains were used to effect a transformation when there was a tapping, dragging sound and a boy came across the stage, leaning on a crutch and carrying a box of flowers. It was difficult to tell how old he was because, while he was no taller than Sara, that was partly because his legs were bowed and undeveloped, but Andrew guessed that he was about fourteen.

"Well, well," said Mrs. Abbott. "Here's Happy Jack again."

"Happy Jack as ever was," said the boy, leaning on his crutch and smiling. "The top of the day to you, Mrs. Abbott. And to you too, Mr. Smollett."

"Hello, Jack," said the stage manager.

"Are those more flowers for Miss de Lille?" asked Mrs. Abbott.

"They are."

"Well, she's changing her clothes, so you'd better let me take them in to her. But don't you go because I'm sure she'll have a little something for you."

"I won't go," said Jack. "I'd never go if I didn't have to."

"I know that," said Mrs. Abbott. "By the way, here are two friends of mine." And she introduced Sara and Andrew.

"Pleased to meet you," said Jack, tugging at the brim of his ragged cap. "Any friend of Mrs. Abbott is royal family to me. But I'm afraid I'm butting in. Am I, Mr. Smollett?"

"No, Jack. I was just showing them how the star trap works and how we fly the scrims—all things you know." At this point one of the stage hands called him, and he excused himself and left.

"Slap up, he is," breathed Jack. "They're all top hole here. Ain't no place on earth like the theatre."

"No, there's not," said Sara. "It's fine out front, but it's wonderful back here, too."

"So t'is," said Jack, beaming at her. "It's like magic out front—not that I ever seed a play all the way through, just bits and pieces. But even when they show you how they did it back here, it's still magic."

"Do you get backstage a lot?" asked Andrew.

"Yes, I do. Work for Foljamb, the florist, I do. Shop right around the corner. We delivers more flowers to theatres than any other florist in London and I'm the one who does it."

"Is that why you like the theatre so much?" asked Sara.

"Maybe part of the reason," said Jack. "But another's because of me mum. She was a actress, she was."

"Would we know her?" asked Andrew.

"I doubts it. It's been a long time since she was in anything. But when she was, she was prime, she was. She played in *Cinderella* and *Robinson Crusoe*, and she was supposed to be principal boy in *Babes in the Wood*, but something happened."

"What was that?" asked Andrew.

"She died."

"I'm sorry to hear that," said Sara.

"Yes," said Jack, nodding. "Sad, it was. Terrible sad. Young she was and pretty, and a great actress she would have been; but that's the way it goes sometimes."

Mrs. Abbott came back out.

"Miss de Lille was very sorry not to see you, Jack, but—like I said—she was changing and a little pushed for time. But she wanted me to give you this." And she gave him some coins.

"Oh, thank 'ee, thank 'ee ever so, Mrs. Abbott. And even more thanks to Miss de Lille. But I'll be seeing her again because as long as the panto keeps playing, the flowers'll keep coming."

"I'm sure they will," said Mrs. Abbott, smiling. "Goodbye to you, then. And goodbye to you too, Sara and Andrew. Will you give my regards to your mother, Andrew? And tell her I hope we'll be seeing her around here very soon."

"I'll do that, Mrs. Abbott," said Andrew. She kissed him with the freedom and gusto of someone who's spent her whole life around the theatre and went back to Miss de Lille's dressing room.

"Excuse me," said Jack. "I couldn't help overhearing what she said about your mum. Is she in the theatre?"

"Well, yes. Though not at the moment."

"Tillett! I wasn't thinking, didn't pay no attention when said your name, but . . . Are you Verna Tillett's son."

"Yes, I am."

"But she's a star—a flat-out famous star! Many's the time I brought her flowers when she was playing at the Windsor in *Jane Eyre*."

"Yes, she was in *Jane Eyre*," said Andrew. "But, as I said, she's not in anything now."

"Where are you for now?" Sara asked Jack, aware that his extreme enthusiasm was making Andrew uncomfortable and trying to change the subject. "Are you going back to the shop?"

"No. There's nowt more to do there, and they told me to go home, so that's what I'll do. Takes me a little time, pegging away on this," he said cheerfully, indicating his crutch. "But I don't mind."

"Where's home?" asked Sara.

"Clerkenwell Road, near Farringdon Street."

"That's just past Gray's Inn," said Andrew. "We'll take you there."

"What do you mean, take me?"

"We've got a carriage waiting for us," said Sara, who had guessed that Andrew would suggest it. "It won't take us out of our way."

"Oh, no, no!" said Jack, drawing back. "You can't do that!"

"Of course we can," said Andrew. "How would you go if we didn't take you? Omnibus?"

"Sometimes if I'm tired or the weather's real bad, I takes the bus. But mostly I just gimps along out there."

"Well, that's ridiculous," said Sara. "Come along now," and they shepherded him across the stage, out the stage door and up the alley like a pair of sheep dogs guiding a balky lamb. Fred was waiting on Drury Lane as they had arranged and didn't seem at all surprised to see their companion.

"Well, I'm glad you didn't hurry on my account,"

he said ironically. "I could have froze for all you cared. Who's your friend?"

"Happy Jack Collins," said Andrew. "He's a fan of my mother's and a great theatre buff and we're going to take him home."

"As long as it's not Bermondsey or Stoke Newington or some place so far I'll be late picking up your mum, I don't mind. Where *is* home?"

"Clerkenwell Road."

"Easy as licking hokey-pokey. In you get."

"But I told you I can't!" said Jack, looking at the brougham with the yellow wheels and gleaming brass lamps. "I've never been in a carriage in my life."

"Then it's time you were," said Sara. "Come on now. Don't keep us and the horses waiting."

Brushing the seat of his pants, Happy Jack lifted himself on his crutch, pivoted skillfully and sank down on the far side of the carriage's rear seat.

"No one's going to believe this!" he said. "Me in Verna Tillett's own carriage!"

"Of course they'll believe it," said Sara. "Why shouldn't they?"

"When we get to the road, you can tell me where to go," said Fred, closing the carriage door.

"Anyplace'll do," said Jack. "The church, the iron foundry . . ."

"We'll take you to your house, wherever it is," said

Andrew. He leaned forward, looking at the crutch that Jack held between his knees. "That's quite a wonderful crutch."

"Ain't it?" said Jack proudly, holding it out so that he could look at it more closely. "Gramps made it for me."

"Gramps?"

"Me mum's father. I lives with him. He was in the theatre too one time. Dabby Dick they called him. Famous he was, the best stage carpenter in London."

"I believe it," said Andrew. The crutch had clearly been made by a first class craftsman. The curved cross-piece that fit under Jack's arm was padded with leather, the oak shaft polished, and its end protected by a metal tip.

"What does he do now?" asked Sara.

"A little carpenting, a little iron work, a little locksmithing and a lot of drinking. He's getting on, not as young as he was, but it's the gin as done him in."

Andrew nodded, aware of how often that sort of thing happened.

"Have you always lived there, on Clerkenwell Road?" he asked.

"Always. Gramps took care of me after mum died. Leastways, he got a woman neighbor to look after me till I was able to go to school. Why do you ask?"

"I was just interested—particularly in the way you

talk, which isn't at all like most people who live in this part of London."

"That's music to my ears, that is—'specially coming from someone like you. Because I made up my mind long ago that, no matter how 'umble you may be—and 'umble I am—you can always better yourself by learning to speak proper. And the place to learn to do that, it seemed to me, was around the theatre—not just from actors and actresses, but from everyone there."

They had gone up Kingsway, cut through the streets behind Gray's Inn and were coming out on Clerkenwell Road.

"Which way now?" called Fred from the box, slowing up.

"Right here," said Jack. "Or across there. Anyplace at all is fine."

"Now stop it," said Sara. "It's late and it's cold. Tell us exactly where you live, and we'll take you there."

"But this is fine," said Jack, squirming in another fit of awkwardness. "You've done enough, more than enough. If you'll just let me out here, on the other side of that warehouse . . . Why, there's Gramps!"

Looking out of Jack's window, Andrew and Sara saw a thin, lantern-jawed man approaching. Wearing a peacoat and a knitted wool cap, he came down the street, tacking a little unsteadily from side to side. He was about to turn into a narrow alley on the far side of the warehouse when he saw the carriage approaching and paused to look at it.

"Gramps!" called Jack, opening the brougham door as Fred pulled up. "Wotcher! It's me!"

"Come off it!" said the old man with an exaggerated scowl. "Maybe you look like me grandson, Jack, but he don't go toffing around in fancy carriages."

"But it is me! It is! It's just . . ." Then seeing the twinkle in the old man's eye, "Ah, you're pulling my leg. I wants you to meet Sara Wiggins and Andrew Tillett. His mother's the actress, Verna Tillett."

"And right rorty she is. My compliments, Master Tillett . . . Miss Wiggins. What are you doing transporting that grandson of mine all over London with you?"

"Met 'em backstage at the pantomime, I did," said Jack excitedly. "I was taking flowers in to Miss Lily de Lille, and there they was talking to Miz Abbott, and she told 'em who I was and—"

"Lily de Lille," said old Mr. Collins. "She's playing in *Aladdin*. Was you seeing it, by any chance?"

"Yes," said Sara. "That's why we were there."

"Then you seen some of my work—which is also some of the best in London. I was at the Drury Lane for seven years, put in the star trap there if you know what that is. *And* worked out the genie effect, his appearing out of a puff of smoke."

"We certainly do know what the star trap is," said

Andrew. "I think that the transformations and some of the effects were the best part of the pantomime."

"Of course they were. And, like I said, mine are the best in London. It's their loss, not mine, that I'm not doing that kind of thing no more."

"Is there any chance that you'll be coming back to the theatre, doing any more stage work?" asked Sara.

"I doubts it. I got enough other things to keep me busy, so I don't need to do that no more. Well, come along, Jacko boy. Thank your friends for bringing you home."

"Oh, I do thank you, I do—most truly and sincerely," said Jack. "And I hopes I has the pleasure and honor of seeing you again sometime."

"I'm sure you will," said Andrew. "Goodbye, Jack. Goodbye, Mr. Collins."

"Goodbye to you," said Collins. "All right, Jacko. Inside with ye and get started on me tea."

Happy Jack turned and stumped up the alley that led to one of the warrens of tenements that you could find all through the area, and old Mr. Collins was about to follow him when there was a shrill whistle from farther up the street.

"Is that you, Dabby Dick?" called a man coming toward him.

"Depends who's asking," said Collins. "Who's that? Oh, it's you. You're early."

"Maybe a touch." The man had reached Collins, set

down the heavy bag he was carrying and looked suspiciously at the brougham that had turned and was now on its way back to the West End. "Who's that?"

"Oh, a pair of young toffs giving themselves good marks for bringing my Jack home from Drury Lane." Then, kicking the bag the man had set down, "Well, you weren't shy about what you brung, were you?"

"No. I thought it could all use a do."

Andrew had looked out as the carriage passed the man, leaned back quickly so he couldn't be seen and, now that they were well up the street, was looking out the window again.

"What is it?" asked Sara. "What's up?"

"Not what. Who. Didn't you recognize the man with the bag, the chap who called out to Jack's grandfather?"

"Not really," said Sara. She tried to look back, but by now the two men had disappeared up the alley. "There was something familiar about him, but . . . Who was he?"

"Nifty Bolan. The cracksman who had just gotten out of jail and was having lunch with Mr. Norwood."

"You're right. But there's nothing wrong with his coming here to see Mr. Collins, is there?"

"I've no idea. I just find it kind of interesting."

"Yes," said Sara thoughtfully. "I suppose it is."

7

A Helping Hand

"Yes?" said Mr. Norwood, looking up from the ledger in which he was writing. "Come in."

The door opened and a seedy-looking man came into the small office. He was unshaven, and his face was sallow and unhealthy. He was probably in his middle thirties. He was wearing a ragged coat that was too big for him and made him look as if he'd lost a good deal of weight.

"You with the Society?" he asked in a hoarse, raspy voice.

"If you mean the Golden Rule Society, yes, I am."

"Right, then. Me name's Clipson. Keegee Clipson."

"And I'm Nicholas Norwood. Sit down, Mr. Clipson, and tell me what I can do for you."

"First off, maybe you'd better tell me if what they say about your Society's true."

"What do they say?"

"That you're in the business of helping old lags."

"Well, I don't know that you can call it a business, but in general that's true. Where did you hear about us?"

"In the clink. Wandsworth."

"You were in Wandsworth?"

"Did four years hard for breaking and entering. And hard it was. I wasn't sure I'd live through it, but I did—just got out yesterday."

"And who told you about the Society?"

"Another lag, name of Tom."

"Tom what?"

"I just knew him as Tom, old Tom. He was in the cell across from me, and we got to be pretty good friends, especially near the end when I got sick."

"What was wrong with you?"

"What *wasn't* wrong! First me stomach went dicky from the food and I couldn't keep nothing down. Then I got the sweats, jail fever, and I started coughing till I was spitting blood."

"That sounds pretty serious."

"Old Tom thought it was. He said I'd probably live to get out, but if I ever came back in I'd be a goner. That's why he thought I should come to see you, see if I couldn't go straight."

"Well, of course we'll do anything we can to help

you. I gather you'd like us to help you get some kind of work."

"That's right. And fast. I'm flat as a flounder."

"I'll let you have something on account, but what kind of work do you think you could do?"

"I don't know. Something to do with tools. I'm good with them because I used to be a cracksman. As a matter of fact, I was probably the best cracksman in London."

"You don't say," said Norwood, smiling. "I've been told that requires a high degree of skill. Well, let me see what I can do. I just placed someone in a machine shop over in Southwark and I may be able to get you a job there too." He pulled over the ledger. "What's your address?"

"Two Arnold Court, Hoxton."

Norwood wrote it in the ledger, then took out his note case. "In the meantime, here's something to keep you going," he said, holding out a pound note.

"I don't want no charity," said Clipson, scowling, "from you or nobody else!"

"It's not charity. It's . . . I suppose you can call it an advance against any money you make when I get you a job. You can pay me back then."

"I say it's charity, and I don't want it!" He got up. "Let me know when you got a job for me."

"I'll do that," said Norwood looking at him seriously and intently. "Have you had lunch?"

"No. Why?"

"If you won't take any money, I'd like to buy you lunch—it's the least I can do. But unfortunately I won't be able to leave until a man from Chubb's gets here, and that won't be for a half hour or so."

"Chubb's, the safe people?"

"Yes."

"What's he coming here for?"

"I got a safe from them the other day." Norwood nodded toward the small safe in the corner of the room. "And they must have given me the wrong combination because, after I put some things in it and closed it, I wasn't able to open it. They're sending a man over to see if he can open it and give me the correct combination."

Clipson walked over to the safe.

"Looks like one of their new ones," he said.

"I believe it is."

Clipson looked up at him.

"Are you a betting man?" he asked.

"I put the odd quid on a horse now and then. Why?"

"I said I don't want no charity—and I don't. But I'll bet you a quid I can open that safe for you—and do it in under five minutes."

"You're on," said Norwood, smiling. He took a large silver watch with a hunting case out of his pocket, opened it and set it on his desk. "Whenever you're ready."

"Oh, I'm always ready," said Clipson, kneeling down in front of the safe. "I don't need tools for a crib like this." He blew on his fingers, rubbed them together and flexed them like a pianist getting ready to go on stage for a concert. "Here goes."

Pressing an ear to the front of the safe and listening intently, he began turning the dial. He turned it around completely once before he stopped and glanced at it. "Once to the right and then to five," he said. He began turning the dial the other way. "Left to nineteen." He turned it to the right again. "One right . . . two right. Two right to twelve." There was a faint click. Clipson turned the handle and pulled on it and the safe swung open. "And bob's your uncle."

"Well, I'll be dashed!" said Norwood. He looked at his watch. "Three minutes and forty seconds."

"Should have done it in less, but I'm a little out of practice. Have you got the right combination now?"

"I believe so," said Norwood, glancing at the pad on which he had written it. Then, handing him the pound note, "I must say I'm impressed. How do you do it?"

"If you've got the gift, like I have, you can tell when the tumblers are lining up. Well, I'll be toddling. You'll let me know if you find something for me?"

"I will. And I think I can assure anyone who might

have an opening that if they hire you, they'll be getting someone top hole."

"Ta!" said Clipson in offhanded thanks. "And ta-ta!"

And he went out, leaving Norwood looking after him with an amused but admiring smile.

8

Beasley and Friends

At about that same time the next day, Sara and Andrew went to visit their old friend, Baron Beasley. Beasley —Baron was a name, not a title, as Peter Wyatt had informed them when he first introduced them—had a store on Portobello Road where he sold antiquities, curiosities, gewgaws and bricabrac. He had a wide ac- quaintanceship with London's less affluent dealers and those who had dealings with those dealers. As a result, though he was rigorously honest himself and would have been outraged if anyone had suggested that he do anything even vaguely illegal, he probably knew more about what was going on in London's seamy side than anyone else in the metropolis. And since he loved food, liked to eat well and interestingly, Sara and Andrew timed their visit so that they would arrive at his shop at lunchtime.

They took a bus to Oxford Street, changed and got off at Pembridge Road and walked to Beasley's shop. The window was much the same as it had been when they had first come there. A Russian samovar and a marble head of Napoleon shared the center and around them were horse brasses, glass paperweights and decorated china doorknobs.

Beasley, large and impassive looking as a Buddha, was behind the counter talking to a swarthy, dark-haired man who wore a green and yellow checked suit with a snuff-colored waistcoat.

"Well, if it's not my two favorite younkers," said Beasley. "How are you, Sara, Andrew?"

"Not too bad," said Sara. "And you?"

"Fine as a fiddle with a new coat of varnish. This Romany looking rom here is Keegee Clipson. Sara Wiggins and Andrew Tillett."

"Greetings and salutations," said Clipson, looking them up and down with a sharp eye. "Are these the friends you said would be having lunch with us?"

"I said friend, not friends. No, Sara and Andrew are lagniappe, if you know what that is."

"Something a little extra."

"Right. I wasn't expecting them, but they're always welcome. Sean," he called to his assistant who was in back of the shop somewhere. "We're off. If you-know-who gets here, tell him we're at Alexis's."

"I'll do that, Mr. Beasley," said Sean, sticking his

head out through the curtain that closed off the rear of the shop. "Season's greetings, Sara and Andrew."

"Same to you, Sean," said Andrew.

They followed Beasley and Clipson out of the shop and up Portobello Road to a restaurant called the Acropolis. Alexis, a smiling man with huge mustachios, embraced Beasley as if he were his long-lost brother, shook hands with Sara, Andrew and Clipson and sat them at a large corner table.

"What kind of a place is this?" asked Clipson suspiciously.

"Greek," said Beasley.

"Greek? What's wrong with good old English cooking? I'll wager I'll not be able to get a cut off the joint here!"

Beasley looked at him scornfully, then turned to Sara and Andrew. "See what I have to put up with? Philistines! We live in one of the great cities of the world, a city rich in culinary variety. And what does this lump and bump want? A cut off the joint!" Then, as Sara and Andrew shook their heads in commiseration, "When you have lunch with me, Clipson, you go where I take you and you eat what I order. *Compris?*" He turned to Alexis. "How's the moussaka?"

"How do you think it is? Ambrosia!"

"All right. We'll have that. And avgolemono soup to start with."

"I bring it to you myself," said Alexis.

"I'm expecting another friend," said Beasley. "I'm not sure when he'll get here, but . . ."

"If I'm not mistaken," said Sara, who was facing the door, "he's here now."

Andrew and Beasley both turned as Wyatt came in. He saw them at the same time that they saw him, scowled as he approached the table.

"What the blue blazes are the two of you doing here?" he asked.

"They're having lunch with me," said Beasley.

"Why today?"

"Why not today? They know they're welcome anytime. Meet my friend, Keegee Clipson. Inspector Peter Wyatt of Scotland Yard."

"What?" said Clipson, bouncing to his feet. "Is this the friend you was talking about? I ain't having lunch with no poxy slop, specially not a crusher!"

"Ah, language!" sighed Beasley. "What riches we can find in common speech. Do you know what he's talking about, Sara?"

"Of course. Used this way, poxy is a derogatory adjective like blinking and blooming. A slop is back-slang for a copper or policeman and a crusher is a plainclothes policeman."

"Well done," said Beasley. Then to Clipson, "Are you impressed?"

"No, I'm leaving!"

"You are not," said Beasley, catching him by the sleeve. "Sit down."

"I told you . . ." said Clipson.

"I know. But you're not having it with him. You're having it with Sara, Andrew and me."

Wyatt, aware that there was more to be gained from silence than from speech, decided not to comment further on the presence of the two young people and sat down without saying another word.

"I don't like it, Beasley," Clipson grumbled. "I don't like it for monkey nuts. I ain't no nark."

"Of course you're not," said Beasley soothingly. "You were just finding something out for a friend of yours. Me."

"Well, all right," said Clipson, sitting down. He was looking sideways at Wyatt when Alexis reappeared with large bowls of steaming soup, set one down in front of each of them.

"What's this?" he asked suspiciously.

"What's it look like?"

"Soup. But what kind?"

"Why don't you taste it and see if you like it?"

Clipson waited until Sara, Andrew and Wyatt had each tasted it and nodded approvingly before he took a tentative mouthful.

"Tastes like there's lemon in it."

"There is."

"I never heard of soup with lemon in it." He took another spoonful. "But t'ain't bad. In fact, it's kind of good." He took several more mouthfuls. "This friend of yours," he said. "The one I don't want to have nothing to do with . . . does he know what you wanted me to do?"

"Since we discussed the whole thing before I spoke to you," said Beasley, "I think maybe he does."

"Hmm," said Clipson. He turned to Sara and Andrew who were sitting together, Sara next to Wyatt. "What Beasley wanted me to do," he told them, "was to go see someone—a chap named Norwood who's got an office on Carnaby Street in Soho."

"Nicholas Norwood of the Golden Rule Society?" said Sara.

"That's the cove. Well, I'd heard a little about him here and there, so I went. He's got a small office up a flight over a draper's shop. A real toff he is. I don't like toffs, but I must say he seemed like a nice one, pleasant and easy like. Well, I give him my pitch, told him I was just out of Wandsworth and I heard if you wanted to go straight, he'd give you a hand."

"And had you been in Wandsworth?" asked Andrew.

"Me?" said Clipson scathingly. "I'm not just good —I'm the best there is, and I ain't been nabbed and in a clink since I was a nipper. Of course, I wasn't dressed this way. I wore duffy duds and had me face

74

fixed so I'd look old and sick and kept holding me guts like they was killing me." And he went on to tell them everything that had happened in Norwood's office, including his opening of the safe.

"It took you three minutes and forty seconds?" said Beasley. "You're slipping, Keegee."

"Come off it!" said Clipson indignantly. "I had to pretend I was out of practice, didn't I?"

"I suppose so," said Beasley. "And that's all that happened?"

"No," said Clipson. "It's not." Then, as Alexis took away the soup plates and put something that looked like a meat pie in front of each of them, "What's this?"

"If I told you it was called moussaka, would that mean anything to you?"

"No." He tasted it. "It's something like shepherd's pie, but it's got something in it that ain't potatoes."

"Eggplant."

"Eggplant? Never even heard of it before, but like the soup, it ain't bad. Where was I?"

"You were going to tell us what else happened."

"Right. It was about noon when I went to see Norwood. Well, last night I was leaving the house to go meet someone at the pub when a four-wheeler pulls up and someone calls to me—a woman."

"Young or old?" asked Wyatt.

Clipson look at him stolidly, then turned back to Beasley.

75

"Did you say something?" he asked.

"Yes. Could you see the woman, tell anything about her?"

"No. She was sitting way back, told me to stay where I was so I couldn't see her clear, but she didn't sound old. Matter of fact, she had a nice voice."

"What did she want?" asked Andrew.

"She said she'd heard I just got out of the clink, needed brass and wanted to know if I wanted to do a little job for her."

"What kind of a job?" asked Sara.

"Cracking a crib. I told her what I'd told Norwood —that I was a sick man and couldn't take a chance on being thrown in the pokey again. She said she understood that, but that this was as safe as houses and that the split would be enough for me to live on for a year. I said I'd have to think about it, and she said I could have a couple of days, and if I changed my mind, I was to pull up one of the curtains in my room and leave the other one down. She pointed out which curtain she meant and drove off."

"In other words, she knew where he lived," said Wyatt.

"We gather she knew where you lived," said Andrew.

"She knew that, all right. And she also knew she didn't want me to know nothing about her. Because she not only sat way back in the growler so I couldn't really see her, but the hack number was covered up so I couldn't read it."

"Ask him if he's sure it was a public hack and not a private carriage," said Wyatt.

"Was it?" asked Sara.

"It was a public hack, the real thing. Not that that don't mean she don't own it."

"It sounds to me as if you did beautifully," said Sara. "Are you really going straight as you said you are?"

"Hah!" He looked belligerently, not at her but at Wyatt. "Why should I go straight? I'm careful enough so that no one's laid a finger on me since I was ten. And I'm good enough so that I only have to work twice a year to live like a king."

"Is he as good as he says he is?" Wyatt asked Beasley. "As good as Nifty Bolan, for instance?"

"Nifty Bolan!" said Clipson angrily. "Things he wouldn't dare touch, I can open with me eyes closed and me hands tied behind me back!"

"You don't say," said Wyatt. "Not that there's likely to be any contest. For the word is that *he's* going straight now."

"He couldn't go straight if he was pulled through a keyhole!" said Clipson. Then, looking suspiciously at Wyatt, he addressed him directly for the first time. "You were having me on, weren't you? What are you up to?"

"Nothing you need worry about," said Wyatt.

"Talking of Bolan," said Andrew. "We saw him yesterday."

"Where was this?"

Andrew told him of their meeting with Happy Jack Collins after the pantomime, of taking him home and meeting his grandfather, and of how Bolan had appeared just as they were leaving.

"You say he was carrying a bag," said Wyatt. "How big a bag?"

"About the size of a good-sized Gladstone. But it was heavy, very heavy."

"That's interesting," said Wyatt. "Everything I've heard here today has been interesting. And even though we've never met or talked," he said to Clipson, "I won't forget it. I owe you one, and I always pay my debts."

"Ah, well," said Clipson. "I didn't do it for you. I did it for old Beasley here. Besides, there's something funny going on—something I don't twig. And what I don't twig, worries me."

"It worries me, too. But maybe the two of us together will be able to get to the bottom of it."

9

The Wicked Flee

Andrew was in the parlor setting up the backgammon board when the bell for the front door jangled. He had begun playing backgammon at school, taught Sara how to play during his last holiday and was now a little sorry that he had, for she had been beating him soundly and consistently. For some time he had insisted that it was just luck—after all, the moves depended on a throw of the dice—but by now he knew there was more to it than that. You could not call it card sense because there were no cards involved, but it was the same sort of instinct, which told her which piece to move, when it was safe to leave a blot and when she had better cover and make the point.

Andrew heard Matson go to the door and open it. There was a brief exchange, then the door closed. Andrew was checking the board to make sure that the pieces were set out correctly when Sara came in.

"I'm sorry I took so long," she said. "Your mother wanted me to look at something."

"A new hat."

"How do you know?"

"When you have spent a lifetime unraveling the secrets of the human soul, my dear," he began in a cracked, old man's voice.

"Oh, poof! You saw the box!"

"Right. Who came in? It's not that newspaper man, is it?"

"No. He's not due here for a while yet. It was some flowers for your mother."

"From Peter?"

"Who else would send her flowers now, when she's not in a play? I mean, it's different when she's playing."

"I know what you mean." Then, as Verna came in carrying a large bunch of flowers wrapped in colored tissue paper, "I see that you still have admirers."

"So it would seem," said Verna, smiling and unwrapping them. "Aren't they beautiful?"

They were roses, some pink, some red, all dewy and fragrant.

"Yes, they are," said Sara. "From Peter?"

"I assume so. Let's see." She found a small envelope, took out the card it contained and read it.

"Mother!" said Andrew as she went pale and dropped the roses. "What is it?"

She read the card again as if to make sure she was not mistaken, then held it out to Andrew with an unsteady hand. He had hurried to her and put an arm around her waist. Taking the card, he read it.

"The wicked flee when no man pursueth," it said, the writing clear, black and strong. "But there is no hiding place. Vengeance is mine, sayeth the Lord."

Andrew glanced at Sara, who was reading it over his shoulder, then ran out into the entrance hall.

"Matson, who brought those flowers—the ones that just came?"

"A boy, Master Andrew. At least . . . Yes, I think you could call him a boy."

"Had you ever seen him before?"

"No. But I'd know him if I saw him again. He was crippled, walked with a crutch."

"Happy Jack!" said Sara, who had followed him out.

"If it is, I can probably catch him," said Andrew and, without waiting to put on a coat, he pulled open the door and ran across the front garden to Rysdale Road. He looked to the right, and there, far up and almost at Wellington Road, he saw a familiar figure stumping along with a crutch. Andrew ran after him, knowing it was going to be a near thing. If an omnibus came along before he got to Wellington Road, Happy Jack would get away. Of course Andrew knew where he worked and where he lived and could always find him, but . . .

"Yoicks! View halloo!" called a voice he knew. "What's up, Andrew?"

It was Wyatt, in a hansom, who had come up behind him, seen him run out of the house and followed him.

"I've got to catch someone, that boy with the crutch up there!"

Wyatt knew him too well to ask any questions.

"Jump in," he said, opening the waist-high leather apron. "Cabby . . ."

"Gotcher, guv'ner," said the cabby as Andrew jumped in. Cracking his whip, he sent the horse up the street at a fast trot.

"What's this about?" asked Wyatt.

Andrew told him, gave him the card, which he had slipped into his pocket. Wyatt read it, and his face became grim.

"You're sure that that's the boy who delivered it?"

"Yes. As it happens, I know him. It's the boy I told you about—the one we took home after the pantomime."

"The one whose grandfather Bolan came to see?"

"Yes."

"Jack!" called Andrew, getting out of the hansom.

Jack, his back to him, whirled and crouched, raising his crutch like a club.

"Who's yer?" he said savagely. "Stand back now! You come any closer, and . . . Why, Master Andrew!"

"Sorry if I startled you."

"It's all right," said Jack, straightening up and tucking the crutch under his arm. "I'm just surprised to see you. I mean, I knew that was your house I was at, but . . ."

"You brought the flowers there?" said Wyatt.

"Yes, sir. I did."

"This is Inspector Wyatt of the Metropolitan Police, Jack," said Andrew. "And this is Happy Jack Collins."

"An inspector? I ain't never met an inspector from Scotland Yard before. Is anything wrong, sir?"

"I'm interested in those flowers you just delivered to Miss Tillett. Where did they come from?"

"Why, from Foljamb, the Covent Garden florist. I works for him. Master Andrew here knows I do."

"I believe you. Do you know who ordered the flowers? Who bought and sent them?"

"No, sir. I don't. I never knows. They just gives me the flowers and tells me where they're to go, and sometimes, when it's a long way like now, they give me sixpence to take a bus."

"I see. Well, of course Foljamb would know."

"Yes, sir. Likely he would. But you still haven't

told me what was wrong. I was very careful with the flowers, sir. I'm always careful, but I was particular careful with these because I'd met Master Andrew here, and besides I think Miss Tillett is wonderful— one of the most wonderful actresses in London."

"There was nothing wrong with the flowers, Jack," said Andrew. "We just wanted to know who had sent them."

"Like I said, I don't know. I never knows. But I'm sure Mr. Foljamb could tell you."

"I hope he can," said Wyatt. "All right, Jack. Thanks." And he got back into the waiting hansom.

"You mean I can go now?" said Jack.

"Yes, of course."

"Oh, thank you, sir. Happen I'll see you again around the Strand one day, Master Andrew."

"It's very likely, Jack," said Andrew, getting into the hansom with Wyatt. "Goodbye."

Jack waved to him, then went stumping up the street toward Wellington Road to get a bus back to Covent Garden.

The hansom took them back to the house, where Wyatt paid the cabby. Matson was waiting for them and took Wyatt's coat. Verna and Sara were still in the sitting room. The roses had been picked up and were lying on a table against the wall. Verna had regained her color, but her face still looked strained.

"Hello, Peter," she said, forcing a smile.

"My darling," he said, going to her. She held out her hands to him and he put his arms around her and embraced her, kissing her on the forehead.

"How are you?" he asked, holding her away from him so he could look at her.

"A bit shaken, but all right. I gather you heard what happened."

"I saw Andrew running up the street, picked him up and he showed me the card."

"Was it Happy Jack?" asked Sara.

"Yes," said Andrew. "We talked to him, but he didn't know who the flowers were from. They were just given to him to deliver."

"I'll look into it," said Wyatt. "I'll talk to Foljamb myself, though I'm afraid he won't be able to tell us much. If he can, it will be the first real lead we've had."

"What about the card?" asked Verna as he took it out and studied it. "Can you tell anything from that?"

"Not really. The card seems fairly ordinary, the kind florists usually use. The handwriting is undoubtedly disguised. I'll show it to our handwriting expert at the Yard, but I doubt if he'll be able to tell us much about it."

"But what's the point of it?" asked Sara. "Why was the card sent to her?"

"To worry her, upset her."

"If that was someone's intention, they've certainly succeeded," said Verna. "Do you want the flowers for any reason?"

"No. They must be from Foljamb's regular stock, and they won't tell us anything either."

"Well, I don't want them around. They give me the creeps. Matson!" she called.

"Yes, madam?" he said, coming in.

"Would you get rid of these flowers for me, please?"

"Yes, madam." And picking them up, by some subtle alchemy—the expression on his face, or the way he carried them—he transformed them from a fragrant tribute to something unpleasant that was worthy only of the dust bin.

"What about what the card said?" asked Andrew.

"That doesn't tell us very much either," said Wyatt. "Two of the phrases are from the Bible, phrases that anyone would be familiar with. However, judging by the handwriting as well as the way the phrases were put together, I get the impression that whoever wrote the note was not illiterate."

"That was my feeling, too," said Andrew.

"And mine," said Verna. "Which I somehow find more frightening than if it had been written by some ignorant fanatic." Her hand went to her bosom as the front door bell rang. "Who's that?" she whispered.

"Probably that newspaperman, Fulton of the *Journal*," said Sara.

"That's right. I'd forgotten about him."

"You don't have to see him," said Wyatt. "If you're still upset about that note—and you have a right to be—then Matson can tell him you're indisposed and you can talk to him some other time."

"No. The note he wrote me was a very nice one, and I'm sure I can manage. I gather you intend to stay while he talks to me."

"That's why I'm here."

"I know. And of course I don't mind. But I'm not sure how he'll feel about it."

"I don't much care. I've been wanting to see him for some time."

"Mr. Edward Fulton," said Matson, opening the door and then standing aside.

Fulton had clearly made an effort to dress for the occasion and did not look nearly as raffish as he had when he talked to Sara and Andrew on Regent Street.

"Good afternoon, Miss Tillett," he began. "It was very good of you . . ." Then, seeing Wyatt, he lost his smile. "Oh, Inspector. I didn't expect to find you here."

"I'm sure you didn't," said Wyatt grimly. "I left several notes for you at the *Journal*, asking you to come and see me at the Yard, but you never did."

"I meant to. I started to come over two or three times, but each time something came up."

"Strange how difficult you found it as opposed to

the times when you wanted to ask me about a case. I'm sure you know what I wanted to talk to you about."

"I'm afraid I don't."

"I wanted to know how you knew about the Meg Morrissey murder, where you got the facts on that."

Fulton shook his head, trying to look apologetic, but somehow looked smug.

"I'm sorry, Inspector. I can't tell you that."

"Can't or won't?"

"Can't. If a journalist doesn't protect his sources— if he reveals where he got his information—he's finished. Because no one will ever trust him again."

"I see," said Wyatt coldly. "All right, Fulton. I'll remember that."

Fulton waited a moment, not sure whether Wyatt was going to say anything else. Then he nodded to Sara, looked at Andrew and turned to Verna.

"As I said, it was very good of you to agree to see me. Though, I must confess, I thought I'd be seeing you alone."

"Inspector Wyatt is an old friend," said Verna in a neutral voice. "I wouldn't dream of asking him to leave."

"I see. Of course I know Miss Wiggins. I saw her just the other day on Regent Street. But I'm afraid I don't know this young man."

"My son, Andrew."

"Oh." Again Fulton hesitated, as if not sure whether Sara and Andrew were going to remain also, but when neither of them made a move to leave, he sighed, took a notebook from his pocket and gave Verna his full attention.

"I wanted to talk to you about your new play, *Thy Name Is Woman*. That is the title, isn't it?"

"Yes."

"There was a good deal of talk about it until just the other day. I know there was a problem about getting a proper theatre, but that was supposedly settled and the word was that you were going into rehearsal, but . . . *Are* you in rehearsal?"

"Not at the moment."

"Will you be going into rehearsal within the next few days?"

"I'm afraid I can't say."

"In other words, no date's been set."

"That's correct."

"Can you tell me why the production's been delayed?"

"Don't you think that's something you should discuss with Mr. Harrison?"

"I tried to. He claimed it was because some work was being done on the play. Some rewriting."

"Why do you say 'he claimed'," said Verna, "as if you're not sure he's telling the truth."

"Because I'm not. He was supposedly very enthusiastic about the play. And so were you. That's why I can't help wondering whether there wasn't another reason for delaying the production."

"What other reason?"

"Well, we have had those murders—three of them, all involving actresses, within the last week or so. Murders that were exactly like a series that took place ten years ago and that were never solved. I couldn't help wondering whether that had anything to do with it. Whether you had postponed going into rehearsal because you felt anxious."

"Why should I feel more anxious than any other actress in London?"

"There's no reason why you should. But since you do seem to be . . . Were you threatened?"

Before Verna could answer—before she could do more than glance at Wyatt—he was on his feet and standing in front of Fulton.

"What made you ask that?" he asked quietly but forcefully.

"It was a natural assumption," said Fulton.

"It was *not* a natural assumption! That question was based on information! Wasn't it?"

"Perhaps," said Fulton, shrinking back in his chair.

"There's no perhaps about it. It had to be based on information. And I want to know what that information was."

"I told you before . . ."

"I know. You have to protect your source. Well, I have something much more important than that to protect—human lives. Not just Miss Tillett's, but possibly others. I believe in a free press. I think that our newspapers are a valuable institution and that they play an important role when they act responsibly. But what you're doing isn't responsible. It's cheap, sensational yellow journalism. You're not interested in any large issue. You're just interested in a story—theatrical tittle-tattle. So I ask you again: What made you come here today? What information brought you here? And if you don't tell me, I'm going to charge you with willfully withholding information necessary to a police investigation. Well?"

"You needn't get so shirty," said Fulton. "I know that it's important. It's particularly important because Miss Tillett's involved, and I happen to think she's one of the best actresses we've got. So . . . Here you are. This came to me at the *Journal* yesterday afternoon." He took a note out of his notebook and handed it to Wyatt.

Wyatt unfolded it, read it, then gave it to Verna. Sara and Andrew read it over her shoulder.

It was written in the same strong hand as the note that accompanied the flowers, and it said, "The murdered players' story was well done. If you'd like an interesting sequel, ask Verna Tillett why she's keeping off the boards. Is she afraid she'll be next? And if so, why? Has she been warned? Or do the wicked flee when no man pursueth?"

"You say you got it yesterday at the *Journal?*" said Wyatt.

"Yes."

"How did it get there? Had it been mailed?"

"No. Someone brought it there, put it in my box."

"I don't suppose anyone noticed who it was."

"No. Too many people go in and out."

"Was the note in an envelope?"

"Yes. Addressed to me. But I didn't keep it. I didn't think it was important."

Wyatt nodded. "The way the reference to the murdered players is phrased, I get the impression that this isn't the first communication you've had from this unknown person. Was it he or she who gave you the information about Meg Morrissey?"

Fulton hesitated a moment, then nodded. "Yes. There was another note before this, put in my box just the way this one was. It mentioned that Meg Morrissey had been found dead under mysterious circumstances, said the police were keeping it quiet and suggested maybe they were afraid it might be the beginning of a series of murders like the ones of ten years ago."

"I don't suppose you kept that note."

"No. We get a lot of tips, most of which turn out to be nothing. I threw the note away before I started looking into the Meg Morrissey murder, found there *was* something to it."

"Did you know about the other, old murders?"

"I vaguely remembered them, but it never occurred to me to connect them with the present ones until I got the note."

"Why do you suppose the notes were sent to you as opposed to any other journalist in London?"

"That's an interesting question—one I've been asking myself."

"And?"

"I don't know. Of course I do cover murder stories as well as the theatre, so I'd be good on a story that involved both. But, besides that, I may have done a little talking in one of the pubs, complaining that things were slow and wishing that something big, like a new Jack the Ripper, would come along."

"And you think that whoever sent you the notes overheard you?"

"Don't you think it's possible?"

"I do. But I think there might be another reason. And that's the fact that you're on the *Journal*, a paper that's not exactly known for its high ethical or journalistic standards."

"Maybe we can't afford them," said Fulton, flushing a little. "What you mean is if I'd been on another paper—the *Times* or the *Guardian*—maybe I wouldn't have written the story when I checked with the Yard and found out you wanted it kept quiet."

"That's right."

"You may have a point."

"The question is: What are you going to do now?"

"You're not going to tell me I can't run *this* story, are you?"

"We do have what is supposed to be a free press here in England. Which means that I can't tell you what you should and what you should not print."

"I know. But you can make it pretty difficult for us if we don't do what you want. Now would you rather I *didn't* write the story?"

"Someone clearly wants you to write it, don't they? Write it and run it?"

"So it seems."

"There's no question about it. They gave you the material for the first story, followed it up with this second note. Generally speaking, when an enemy wants you to do something, you should be sure you don't do it. But in this case, we not only don't know who our enemy is, we don't know what he or she is up to. So my feeling is, go ahead. Let's do what he or she wants. Perhaps that will help us determine why he or she wanted the story run."

Fulton sighed with relief. "All right. Is there any special way you'd like it handled?"

"No. Except that it might be well if you weren't

too flat-footed about it. Speculate about whether Miss Tillett might or might not have received some kind of threat without coming out and saying she had."

"Will do," said Fulton, getting up. "Miss Tillett, I'm sorry if I upset you, and I hope the inspector gets to the bottom of this very soon. I feel we're all deprived when you're not on a stage somewhere in London."

"Thank you," said Verna, forcing a smile.

"Well?" said Wyatt after Fulton had left. "Does anyone have anything to say?"

"I liked him better at the end than I did at the beginning," said Sara. "I suppose because he admitted he'd gotten those notes and also because he did seem to care about what happened to Miss Tillett."

"Right," said Andrew.

"Then you feel he was telling the truth about the notes?" said Wyatt. "That he didn't write them himself?"

"That never occurred to me," said Verna. "Don't *you* think that they were legitimate—that they were sent to him?"

"Frankly, I do," said Wyatt. "But no one's infallible, and I like to consider every possibility. Have any of you anything more to say about either of the notes —the one on the card that came with the flowers or the one Fulton just gave me?"

"Well, we agreed that whoever wrote the card was

both literate and intelligent," said Andrew. "There was nothing in the other note to make me change my mind about that."

"No," said Sara. "But there was something else. I'm not sure why, but I have the feeling that whoever wrote them has something to do with the theatre."

"That's interesting," said Wyatt. "And I agree. I suspect that one of the things that gave you that impression was the phrase in the letter Fulton got at the *Journal*: that he ask Verna Tillett 'why she's keeping off the boards.' That sounds like a theatre person talking." Then, as they nodded, "To sum up, it's our impression that the notes were written by someone literate and intelligent who has—or has had—some connection with the theatre."

"But why?" asked Verna. "Why has he or she picked me as a target? I thought you were being silly, all of you, when you worried about my going on in a play. But now . . . now, very frankly, *I'm* worried. Do you think that the person who has been writing the notes is the same person who has been committing the murders?"

"I don't know," said Wyatt. "I'm quite sure there's a connection; but so far I don't know what it is. As for being worried, I can't say, 'Don't be.' But at the same time, I'm sure you know that we're going to do everything we can to protect you. And when I say everything, I mean everything."

"I'm sure you do," said Verna. Then, as he picked up her hand and kissed it, "Where are you going?"

"Back to the Yard. I want some of our experts to look at these notes, see what they have to say about the handwriting, the paper, the ink."

"Will you be coming back?"

"Have you forgotten that we're going to the opera?"

"No. I just wasn't sure . . ."

"My dear!" He bent down and kissed her again, her cheek this time. "We're not going to let this madman —or madwoman—keep us from doing the things we enjoy. I'll see you at a little after seven."

Verna came home at about eleven thirty that night. Andrew had been asleep, but sleeping very lightly, for he woke when he heard Matson open the door and heard Wyatt's voice. Then, about a half hour later, he heard Wyatt leave and Verna come upstairs, after saying goodnight to Matson, who now went through the house for the last time, making sure that all was secure. Andrew should have been able to sleep now. After all, Verna was home and all was well. But though he did drift off again, he did not sleep any more soundly than he had while he was waiting for Verna to come home.

He woke with a start, not knowing what had wakened him. He picked up his watch, which he kept on the table next to his bed. It was a repeater, so there was no need for him to strike a match to see what time it was. He pressed the button next to the winding stem and it chimed once for one o'clock, twice for two quarter hours and three times for another three minutes. It was one thirty-three. He listened. The house was quiet except for the creaking, settling sounds it always made during the night. Then he saw the faint light that showed under the bottom of the door and realized that the light must still be on in Verna's room. Had she fallen asleep with it on? Perhaps. But perhaps not.

Getting out of bed, he stepped into his slippers, put on his robe and crossed the hall to the door of Verna's room, which was directly opposite. Again he listened. There was no sound from within but, when he knocked very lightly, she responded instantly.

"Andrew?"

"Yes, Mother."

"Come in, dear."

He opened the door and went in. She was sitting up in bed wearing a dressing gown, holding a book on her lap, but he had a feeling she had not been reading.

"I saw that your light was on," he said, "and I wanted to make sure you were all right."

"I'm fine. I was just having trouble getting to sleep, so I thought I'd read for a while. What about you?"

"I was asleep, but I woke up. How was the opera?"

"Wonderful. As you know, it's one of my favorites."

"Yes. Did you see anyone there, meet anyone?"

"Lawrence Harrison and his wife. They had some guests with them."

"Did Peter have anything to say? About the notes or the flowers, I mean."

"Not really. He sent someone to Foljamb's to inquire about the flowers. Foljamb himself didn't take the order; he knows me and would have taken special note who placed it. One of the assistants took it at a time when they were very busy. He told the constable he's not sure who placed the order, but he thinks it might have been a woman."

"A woman?"

"Yes. I don't know why anyone should hate me and want to harm me. But, in a way, I suppose it's more likely to be a woman than a man."

"Why do you say that?"

"Well, I don't *think* I've ever done anything to make an enemy of a man. But some woman might resent the fact that I once got a part instead of her."

"But it's been *years* since you had to compete with anyone for a part."

"Well, if whoever's behind the notes and the killings isn't completely rational—and clearly he or she can't be—then time doesn't matter. A grievance can continue to be pressing for years."

"I suppose that's true." He looked at her thoughtfully. "You're upset, anxious, aren't you?"

"Yes, Andrew, I am. Frankly, it surprised me that I should feel this way. There have been times in the past when I worried about something—you, for instance, when you were sick. Or about how I was going to do in a new part. But this is different. I was annoyed to begin with when Peter insisted I stay off the stage until this whole thing was solved. I thought he was being silly, which is very unlike him. But since I got that note with the flowers . . . I think what I find frightening is the fact that it has become personal. It's not just that there's something menacing out there, someone who's killed several other women and might want to hurt me. Someone out there *knows* me, has been thinking of me—and thinking of me in a very special way. 'By the pricking of my thumbs, something wicked this way comes.'"

"That's *Macbeth*, isn't it?"

"Yes."

Andrew moved to the window and was looking out toward Rysdale Road. "Have you looked out of the window since you came home?"

"No. Why?"

"A constable usually comes by here two or three times during the night. But tonight there's been a policeman out there all evening. He goes back and forth as if he's walking a beat, but he's never left Rysdale Road."

"Let's see." She got out of bed and stood there next

to him, watching as the sturdy, helmeted figure in dark blue went by, visible for a moment in the yellow glow of the gaslight and then disappearing in the darkness beyond it. "Is that Peter's work?"

"Of course. If he thought you were in danger and needed protection, he'd see that steps were taken to protect you, no matter who you were. But feeling as he does about you . . . Well, you can imagine that the steps he's taken are probably quite extraordinary."

"I'm sure that's true. And I wonder if that can have anything to do with the way I feel."

"What do you mean?"

"We haven't talked much about your father. You didn't know him—you couldn't since he died before you were born—but he was a wonderful man, and I loved him very much."

"I'm sure you did."

"I was miserable for a long while after he died. When I started to do well in the theatre, that helped. And when I came back from America after all those years and found you, that made even more of a difference. These past few years have been very good ones, and I've been very happy. There was one kind of happiness, however, I never expected to have again: finding a man I could love as much as I did your father, a man who would love me as he did. Then I met Peter. Our feelings for one another have grown over a long period of time. And now . . . Well, as you know, I do love him. Love him as much as I did your father."

"And you feel guilty about it—as if that's wrong, somehow."

"Yes."

"I don't think it's wrong. And I don't think my father would have thought so either."

"Why do you say that?"

"If he loved you, he wouldn't have wanted your life to end when he died. He would have wanted you not just to go on, but to be as happy as possible. And loving someone is a very important part of that."

She looked at him for a moment, her eyes very large and very luminous.

"Yes," she whispered finally. "You're right. Thank you, Andrew."

10

Questions

The summons came the next afternoon, and when it did, neither Wyatt nor Tucker were surprised. They were both in the office, Wyatt writing a report and Tucker doing some filing, when there was a knock on the door and a sergeant came in and gave Wyatt an official-looking note.

Tucker watched him as he read it.

"From his nibs?" he asked.

"If you mean the assistant commissioner, yes." He looked up at the sergeant. "I thought I was his nibs."

"When I'm talking to someone else, you are. When I'm talking to you, it's the assistant commissioner."

"And what's the commissioner?"

"Being just a 'umble sergeant, I wouldn't dream of calling him anything but commissioner. What's he want?"

"To see me."

"When?"

"Now. Right now."

"Oh." Then, dryly, "I wonder why."

"No, you don't."

"Of course, I don't." Then, as Wyatt stood up and straightened his tie, "I want you to listen to your old uncle Tucker for a minute. We've got a very difficult problem here, and, while we may not have come up with any brilliant answers yet, no one else could have come up with anything either. So don't take any guff from old grumble-guts."

"Can I quote you on that?"

"You can."

Smiling, Wyatt left. But the smile did not last long, and by the time he had gone down one flight of stairs and traversed the long corridor that took him to the assistant commissioner's office, he was properly sober. He knocked and went in.

The assistant commissioner's office was in one of the round towers that formed the corners of the facade of New Scotland Yard. Two of the windows faced the Thames and Her Majesty's Indian warehouses on the Surrey side, and the other two looked south at Westminster Bridge and the House of Parliament. Assistant Commissioner Sutton, stocky and square-shouldered with greying hair and a closely trimmed grey beard, was sitting at his desk. Slouched in a chair next to it was a trim, light-haired man in his early forties, who wore his dark coat and striped trousers with great casualness.

"Oh, there you are, Wyatt," boomed the assistant commissioner. "Good of you to come so promptly. I don't believe you know Felix Barnett of the Home Office, do you?"

"No," said Wyatt. "I've never had the pleasure." He did not add that he knew a great deal about Barnett, who was Undersecretary and responsible to the Home Secretary and Her Majesty's government for the proper functioning of the Metropolitan Police.

"No, we never met," said Barnett. "But of course I've heard a good deal about you from friends in the Foreign Office."

"That would have been in the matter of young King Alexander of Serbia," said the assistant commissioner, nodding. "Good show, that."

"Very. It was largely because of that case that I endorsed the decision to give you the responsibility for protecting the Ghazipur jewels."

"Thank you," said Wyatt.

"No need to thank me. You're a very useful member of the force and generally quite sound. Which is one of the reasons I'm so interested in these observations of yours." He held up a sheaf of papers in an official folder.

"Are those my comments on the semi-annual report, sir?" Wyatt asked the assistant commissioner.

"Yes," said Sutton. "I only had a chance to read it this morning, and when Mr. Barnett got here, I gave it to him to look at."

"As I understand it," said Barnett, "it's your conviction that something very disturbing is happening in criminal London. You seem to think that over the past six or eight months, someone has begun to organize a good deal of criminal activity—becoming a kind of czar of crime."

"That is correct, sir."

"I gather you base this hypothesis on the statistics in our own report. On the fact that, though there have been fewer robberies of all sorts, there have also been fewer apprehensions and fewer convictions. In other words, though in general there has been less crime, a greater percentage of the crimes that took place have been successful."

"Exactly so."

"You know this is an old story. Periodically, whenever the gutter press has nothing else to write about, they suggest that some criminal genius has arisen and is playing the tune to which all lawbreaking London is dancing."

"I know that, Mr. Barnett. But this is different."

"Different how?"

"Are you a fisherman?"

"I've done a certain amount of fishing."

"Did you ever fish a pool that was not particularly likely—because it was the wrong time of day or because the water was too high or too low—and still, the minute your line hit the water, you knew that there was something there, something very big, looking over your offering."

"You're saying that you've been sensing something like that?"

"Yes, sir. I and a few others here at the Yard sense that something's going on. And I must say I had that feeling before the most recent report came out and I had a chance to look at the figures."

"Well, as I said, I think it's very interesting. Though of course the only way you'll be able to prove your thesis is if you actually come up with the arch criminal. But that's not why I came over here. I assume you saw this afternoon's *Journal*," he said, nodding toward the copy of the paper that lay on the assistant commissioner's desk.

"I did," said Wyatt, his voice dropping.

"What do you think of that Fulton story?"

"I'd like to say, I think about it as little as possible. But I'm afraid it's too serious a matter to joke about. Of course, I've been expecting it."

"Expecting it?"

"I knew Fulton was writing it. He came out to St.

John's Wood to talk to Verna Tillett yesterday, and I arranged to be there at the time. There was some information he had that I wanted."

"Was he cooperative?"

"He was."

"I gather you were not able to dissuade him from writing the story."

"Actually, I didn't try. Though I often don't like the result, I think it's a mistake for anyone to interfere with the right of the press to print what it wishes."

"I agree. Though I must say that the whole situation is becoming more and more frightening. I mean, for Verna Tillett, one of our most distinguished actresses, to be singled out and specifically threatened . . ."

"I know," said Wyatt, grimly.

"What about the last part of the story where Fulton discusses Sarah Bernhardt's imminent visit and wonders if *she* might be in danger from this mad murderer; did he say anything to you about that?"

"No, he didn't. But it didn't surprise me that he put it in the story. The fact that Madame Bernhardt is coming here has been known for some time."

"Yes. Well, apparently the fact that she might be in danger occurred to others beside Fulton. Here's the real reason I came over to the Yard this afternoon—this note that was sent over to me this morning." He handed Wyatt an official-looking white envelope that was date-lined Paris and had apparently been sent to the Foreign Office by diplomatic pouch.

Wyatt read it and felt himself flush with anger. It was a letter from the First Secretary of the British Embassy to the head of the Foreign Office's French Section. It began by saying that the ambassador had been too angry to write the letter himself, but nevertheless felt it had to be written. It concerned a communication the ambassador had just received from the French Bureau of Foreign Affairs, referring to the Sarah Bernhardt visit and expressing a certain amount of concern for her safety. While they had the greatest respect for the British police, the French had said, in conclusion, Madame Bernhardt was such an important citizen of France that they hoped their British colleagues would not hesitate to call on them for help in protecting her if they felt it was necessary.

"No comment," said Wyatt, handing the note back to Barnett.

"You have better control of your temper than I have," said the assistant commissioner. "I had several comments to make. The nerve of them even to suggest that we might need help to protect this divine Sarah of theirs!"

"The gall of the Gauls?" said Wyatt.

"Very good," said Barnett. "Still, the matter is one that can't be ignored. It's much too serious and would be even if Madame Bernhardt were not coming over. That's why I was lukewarm about this crime lord theory of yours. It's very interesting, but the most important problem we face today is that of those theatrical killings. Famous as Bernhardt is, doesn't Verna Tillett mean as much to us as Bernhardt does to the French?"

"There's no need for you to press that point," said the assistant commissioner. "Not to Inspector Wyatt. He would of course be doing his best to solve the murders and protect Verna Tillett if she were a complete stranger. But, as I understand it, she happens to be a friend."

"Oh. I wasn't aware of that," said Barnett. "Is that true, Inspector?"

Wyatt nodded, seeing no need to tell either of them just how good a friend she was.

"Then I feel more reassured than ever about the matter," said Barnett. "More certain that we have the right man in charge of the case. When is Madame Bernhardt due?"

"She's arriving tomorrow," said Wyatt. "Staying at the Langham. But of course the first big moment—until she actually opens—will come the night after tomorrow when Henry Irving is giving a reception for her at the Lyceum."

"You'll be there?"

"I'll be there."

"And Verna Tillett?"

"She'll be there, too."

"Then I'm sure I need concern myself no further about the matter. That I can assure the Home Secretary that you have it well in hand."

Wyatt bowed. "Is there anything else?"

"I don't think so," said Barnett. "Except . . . of course I'm going to see Bernhardt when she opens at the Gaiety. I saw her the last time she played here in London and it was a memorable experience. But I've never met her. Do you think I might come to the reception, too?"

"I'm sure Henry Irving will be delighted to have you. I'll mention it to him and arrange to have you meet both Madame Bernhardt and Verna Tillett."

"That's very good of you. Thank you."

"Not at all." And bowing again, Wyatt left.

At about the time that Wyatt, doing his best to control his annoyance, was leaving the assistant commissioner's office, Andrew was standing in front of a counter in a shop on Oxford Street, looking at a pair of ladies gloves.

"Are you sure?" he asked Sara.

She sighed. "You asked me what I thought she'd like, and I told you."

"And she's your mother, so I guess you'd know. It's just that a Christmas present should be something you'd never buy for yourself. And I'm sure she does buy herself gloves."

"Black, practical ones, not French ones like these. The only reason I hesitated was because they're so expensive."

"Not for your mother they're not. Very well," he said to the elderly sales clerk. "We'll take them."

"Yes, sir," she said, smiling, and wrapped them up.

Andrew paid for the gloves, then he and Sara went out and stood there for a moment, looking at the crowds that thronged Oxford Street, going into the shops and bazaars and coming out with packages and bundles wrapped in colorful paper and tied with gold or colored ribbons.

"What do you want to do now?" asked Andrew.

"What time is it?"

"Four thirty."

"Too early for tea."

"*And* too early to go home. Shall we walk around a bit?"

"If you like. Though I must say I don't really feel like it."

"Neither do I. And I don't know why."

"Of course you do," said Andrew. "All the people we see around here, going in and out of shops, are thinking of just one thing—Christmas and the presents they're going to give and get. And while we've made ourselves think about that, most of the time we've been thinking about something else. At least, I have."

"Your mother. That note that came with the flowers and that story in the paper."

"That's right."

"But it's not as if nothing's being done about it, Andrew. You know that Peter's been thinking about it constantly and is doing everything he can to protect her and catch the killer."

"I know. And I'm sure that eventually he will catch him or her. But in the meantime . . . Well, I just wish there was something we could do."

"What can we do that the police haven't done? They've been everywhere in the theatre district for days now, in uniform and in plain clothes, talking to everyone who might know anything about the killings or who might have seen or heard something suspicious. Unless we could find someone they haven't talked to or who might not have told them things that he or she knows—" She broke off suddenly and turned to look at Andrew.

"You're thinking about Happy Jack."

"Yes. He's around the theatres more often than anyone else. If the police talked to him—"

"Sara, you're right! If he were asked properly, he might know something—something he doesn't even realize he knows! And, in any case, I think we should let him know what's going on and get him to help us."

"To Foljamb's then?"

"To Foljamb's."

With more enthusiasm than they had felt all day, they went east on Oxford Street, took a shortcut through Soho and crossed Charing Cross Road where, even at this time of year, there were browsers at the stalls in front of the booksellers. They went past the other St. Paul's and there, ahead of them, was Covent Garden. The arcades were quiet now—they only came alive after midnight when the vans and lorries loaded with fruit and vegetables came in and made it the noisiest and most lively spot in London. But of course the smell persisted, the smell that was a heady blend of fruits and flowers.

They stood there for a moment, frowning at Floral Hall, which, like all the other halls, was closed now.

"It must be somewhere around here," said Sara. They walked around the hall, and there it was on a side street, an unlikely place for such a well-known florist. The shop was quiet and empty. A large, red-faced man in a striped apron was helping a starched-looking, grey-haired lady pick over and cut the flowers that were left in the vases.

"Yes, miss, young sir," he said cheerfully. "What can I do for you?"

"We're looking for Happy Jack," said Sara.

"Not here. Gone for the day."

"Oh. Isn't it a bit early?"

"Not a *bit* early—*much* too early," said the woman. "But that's Foljamb for you."

"The boy was sick," said the red-faced man. "Wasn't well to start with and had a wicked, sniffly cold. Besides, things were very slow. Nothing much to do."

"Nothing? *We're* doing things, aren't we?"

"Well, I let him go and I'm not sorry and now shut up about it!" Then, turning to Sara and Andrew, "Want me to give him a message when he comes in tomorrow?"

"Thank you, no," said Andrew. "We know where he lives. We'll go see him there."

"Suit yourself," said the man. He picked up a rose. "Here," he said, giving it to Sara. "Take this to go with your pink cheeks."

"Why, thank you," said Sara, putting it into one of the buttonholes of her coat. "By the way, how long has he been with you?"

"Happy Jack? About four months. One of our customers—a good customer—brought him around and said he needed a job. We weren't too keen about it. He's not what you call nimble, you know. But the boy who'd been with us took off and never came back, so we took Jack on. And I can't say I've been sorry."

"Well, I have," said the grey-haired woman. "He gets around, but he makes you feel like a slave-driver for sending him here and there. Besides, there's something a little smarmy about him—always being so everlastingly grateful for this and that."

"Well, what's wrong with being grateful?" said Foljamb, if that's who it was. "You want him to be *un*grateful?"

"No. Just a little more middling about it."

"Middling! How can you be middling about something like that?"

As the two continued their argument, which seemed to be an old one, Sara and Andrew left, went over to the Strand where they caught a bus, got off at Theobald's Road and walked the rest of the way. Just before they reached Happy Jack's corner, they passed a bake shop, and Sara said, "How would it be if we brought him a little something for his tea?"

"You do get ideas, don't you?" said Andrew. "Let's."

They went in and, after some discussion, passed up the penny buns and jam tarts and ended up with a slice of lardy cake, all sugared and stuffed with raisins and heavy enough to sink a man-of-war.

They went around the warehouse on the corner and up the alley into which Happy Jack had disappeared when they took him home. Andrew had lived in a place very much like this for a short while when he first came to London, but he had forgotten how vile an alley like this could smell. Slipping on garbage and filth and stumbling over bits of bricks and broken bottles, they made their way up the alley and out into a small courtyard surrounded by dilapidated houses. A young girl, younger than Sara, stood in the open doorway of one of them with a baby, a younger brother or sister, in her arms. She looked at Sara with wide, wondering eyes.

"We're looking for Happy Jack," said Sara. "Do you know where we can find him?"

The girl stepped aside and nodded toward a door at the rear of the dark hall. She and the baby, who was sucking on a rag, watched as Sara and Andrew went down the hall, past the rickety stairs and knocked on the door. There was a dragging sound, the tap of the crutch.

"Get out of it now!" said an angry voice. "Off with you, or I'll bash you proper!"

"Jack," said Sara.

"What? Who's that?"

"Sara and Andrew."

"Who?"

"Sara and Andrew."

A bolt was pulled, the door opened, and Happy Jack stood there, leaning on his crutch and staring at them with his mouth open.

"Hello," said Andrew. "We stopped at Foljamb's

to see you, but they said you were sick and had gone home, so we thought we'd come out here."

"We brought you a little something," said Sara, giving him the lardy cake that was wrapped in brown paper. "For your tea."

"No," said Jack. "I don't believe it. I thought it was someone from across the court to pester me, but . . . You come all the way out here to see me, old Happy Jack?"

"Why, yes," said Sara. "Why should that surprise you?"

"Surprise ain't the word. Flabbergasted is more like it. Why should I expect anything like this from someone like you?"

"I wish you wouldn't do that," said Andrew, a little sharply, "act like we're something special and you're not."

"But you are! You're very special—as special a pair as I ever met." Then, reacting to Andrew's frown, "All right. I'll say no more. This ain't much of a place we got here, Gramps and me. Nothing like your place what I seen in St. John's Wood. But come in. Come in."

They followed him into the room, a long, narrow one with a single window that faced the back of the warehouse. There was a bed in an alcove, a cot against the wall and a table with some chairs around it in the middle of the room. And in the far corner of the room, a workbench with some tools on it. The table and chairs were in good repair and looked as if they had been homemade. Though a fire smoldered in the grate, the room was cold.

"Sit down. Please sit," said Jack. "Them chairs is comfortable—Gramps made them hisself." He unwrapped the package Sara had given him. "Lardy cake! Oh, I does love lardy cake! Would you like some? Wouldn't take me long to boil up water for tea."

"Thank you, no," said Sara. "We brought it for you."

"If you're sure, I'll have some now and save the rest for Gramps when he comes home." He tore off a large piece and crammed it into his mouth.

"We said we wanted to see you," said Andrew. "And we did want to. But we also wanted to ask you something."

Chewing and swallowing, Jack waved a hand to indicate he was listening, but Andrew waited till he had swallowed what was in his mouth.

"Go ahead and ask," said Jack finally. "If there's anything I can tell you or do for you, I'd be pleased and proud, I would."

"All right. You probably know about the deaths that have been taking place around the theatres lately— killings, actually."

"Killings?"

"You must have heard about them," said Sara.

"Three actresses have been killed—murdered—at different times during the last few weeks."

"I heard something about it," said Jack, wiping his mouth with the back of his hand. "I don't think I knew there was three of them."

"Well, there were," said Andrew. "The third one took place just the other day—Meg Morrissey near the Garrick where she was playing."

"Meg Morrissey!" said Jack, his mouth open and his eyes wide. "Why, I knew her! I took her flowers right after *The Girl From Fiji* opened!"

"She was the last, killed just a few days ago. Now you know my mother's an actress."

"Indeed I know. Verna Tillett. A great actress she is. A star!"

"Well, we're worried about her. We have reason to believe that someone might be wanting to hurt her."

"But why? Why would anyone want to hurt a wonderful actress like her?"

"Why did anyone want to hurt any of the actresses who were killed? The police think it may be someone who's off his chump—like Jack the Ripper, say. Now you're around the theatres all the time. You know and talk to a lot of people, and what we wanted to ask you was: Is there anything you can tell us—anything you've seen or heard—that would help us find out who was doing the killings?"

Slowly Jack shook his head. "No. I ain't seen or

heard nothing. Like I said, I just heard a little about it, didn't even know that it was three actresses what had been killed."

"Well, if you do hear anything," said Sara. "Hear or see anything, will you let us know? There are lots of people who don't want to get mixed up with the police. But if you let us know, we'd take care of it. We'd get word to the police."

"Why, yes, Miss Sara. I certainly will let you know. I'd be happy and proud if I could help."

The door opened and old Mr. Collins—Dabby Dick —came in.

"Well, what's all this?" he said cheerfully. "Company?"

"Yes, Gramps. You remember Master Andrew and Miss Sara what brought me home in Verna Tillett's own carriage the other day. Well, they just come to see me again, and they brung us a big cut of lardy cake."

"Lardy cake, eh? We'll have it for our tea. Blow up the fire, boy. Throw on a handful of coal and get that kettle boiling."

"Yes, Gramps. I'll do that." And taking some lumps of coal from a pail that was used as a scuttle, he dropped them on the fire and bent down to blow the ash-covered coals to a hotter flame.

"You'll stay and have some tea with us, won't you?" said old Mr. Collins.

"No, thank you," said Sara. "We'd better be getting along home."

"Yes, we had," said Andrew, moving toward the door. The carpet bag that Nifty Bolan had given Mr. Collins the night they brought Happy Jack home was on the floor near the door. Andrew had seen it as soon as they came in and had seen Sara looking at it. Now he deliberately tripped over it.

"Ooh, ow!" he said, just barely keeping himself from falling.

"That blinking bag of Nifty's!" said Mr. Collins, walking over and picking it up. "Are you hurt?"

"No," said Andrew, rubbing his shin. "But whatever's in the bag is very heavy and very hard."

"Tools," said Mr. Collins, setting the bag down near the table and opening it.

"Tools?"

"Yes. Hammer and chisel," he said, taking them out of the bag. "A jack that'll force apart iron bars. Drills, specially hardened and sharpened. And this," he said, holding up a particularly odd-looking drill, "is a petter cutter. It'll go through iron like cheese, even steel, and cut a lock out like taking the eye out of a potato."

"What kind of tools are they?" asked Sara. "A locksmith's?"

"Why, yes," said Collins, laughing and putting them back in the carpet bag. "I suppose you could call them that. A very special kind of locksmith, though. A cracksman. Know what that is?"

"Yes," said Andrew. "A man who breaks open safes. But why have you got them here?"

"They were give to me by a friend who don't need them no more. So he says."

"And what will you do with them?" asked Sara.

"Why, I don't know. They're good tools, and I like tools. I been taking care of them, oiling them and sharpening them. I'll probably find a use for them someday."

"Well, goodbye," said Sara, opening the door. "It was nice to see you again, Mr. Collins. And to see you, Jack."

"It was prime to see you again," said Happy Jack. "Thanks for the lardy cake. And I'll keep my eyes and ears open for what you asked me about."

"Good-o!" said Andrew.

They went out, along the alley and around the corner, and it was only when they were on Clerkenwell Road that they stopped and looked at one another.

"Well, what do you think?" said Andrew.

"You did that well," said Sara, "falling over the bag that way. And it looks as if Nifty Bolan was telling the truth. I mean, he must be going straight if he gave old Mr. Collins his burglar tools."

"Maybe. What about the rest?"

"Our asking Jack to let us know if he hears or sees anything that might help us find the killer? He said he would."

"Yes, I know that that's what he *said*."

She looked at him sharply. "But you don't think he will?"

"I don't know."

"There's certainly something strange about him—very strange. And now that you've brought it up, I'm not sure how much he'll help us either."

11

The Divine Sarah

Wyatt arrived at the house shortly after Sara and Andrew got home. They were in the sitting room with Verna when his hansom drew up outside. Even before Matson opened the door and they heard his voice, Verna seemed to know who it was. She had been sober, quiet. But now her face lit up and there was a glow about her, a warmth in her eyes, that Andrew had not often seen there before.

"My dear," she said when he came in.

"How are you?" he said, going directly to her and taking her hands.

They remained that way for a moment, he standing in front of her and holding her hands and Verna staring up at him. At first both of them seemed content with that, merely looking at one another. Then Verna smiled.

"Is that all the greeting I get?" she asked.

"Would anything more be proper?"

"Quite proper."

Bending down, Wyatt kissed her and again they looked long and searchingly at one another before he straightened up.

"Good evening, Sara. Good evening, Andrew," he said with deliberately excessive formality. "I trust you are both well."

"We are," said Sara, smiling.

"You're staying for dinner, aren't you?" said Verna.

"I'd very much like to."

"Good." She rang for Matson, asked him to tell Mrs. Simmonds that, as they had hoped, Inspector Wyatt would be staying for dinner.

"Any news?" asked Sara when Matson had left.

"News about what?"

"You know very well about what!"

"Yes, I think so. And no, I can't say that there is any news. There's been a development that I think we should discuss. In fact, it's one of the reasons I came here tonight. But we haven't made any major discovery, turned up anything that changes the general situation. What about you?"

"I'm glad you asked that," said Verna. "Our young friends here have been up to something. They were just starting to tell me about it when you arrived."

"Oh?" said Wyatt. "Tell."

Taking turns, Sara and Andrew reported on their visit to Happy Jack, telling what they had asked him and what they had asked him to do and then going on to Jack's grandfather's arrival and an account of what was in Nifty Bolan's bag and what Mr. Collins had to say about it.

"Doesn't that mean that what Bolan told you was the truth?" said Sara. "That he is going straight?"

"Not necessarily. There's another possible explanation for it."

"What's that?" asked Andrew.

"We've more important things than that to discuss," said Wyatt, and he told them about his meeting with the assistant commissioner and his talk with Barnett of the Home Office.

"The French wanted to send men over to help guard Madame Bernhardt?" said Andrew incredulously.

"Yes."

"What did you say?" asked Sara.

"I said I thought we could manage without them."

"Politely?" asked Verna, smiling.

"As politely as I could. Which I suppose was not very. And that brings us to the important question. As you know, the reception is the night after tomorrow at the Lyceum. Are you going to it?"

"Well, of course I've been invited. And I had planned to go. Do you think I shouldn't?"

Wyatt looked at her—at her and beyond her at contingencies that none of them could begin to imagine. His face became strained, and Andrew knew that he was weighing the question as seriously as a surgeon does a sudden development during an operation.

"Yes," he said finally. "I think you should go. But on one condition. That Andrew and Sara go, too."

This was so unexpected that they stared at him. And Verna didn't just stare, she laughed.

"What a strange condition to make! Not that I mind. I think it's a very nice idea, and I'm sure it can be arranged. But why?"

"Because they're bright, they have sharp eyes and there's no one else in the world—besides me—who is as concerned about you and your safety as they are."

"Then you think there might be some danger in my going?"

"The terrible part of all this is that there's going to continue to be danger—and not just for you—until we catch whoever is responsible for these murders. Yes, you could be in danger at the reception. But you could also be in danger if you didn't go and stayed home here. And since I *have* to be at the reception, I think that—on balance—you should go too—with the proviso I made."

"That Sara and Andrew go, too." She looked at them. "How do you feel about it? Would you mind?"

"Do you really mean that?" said Sara who had become pale with excitement. "That we can come with you and see, maybe even meet, Sarah Bernhardt?"

"Yes, Sara. I'll send a note to Mr. Irving." She glanced at Andrew, then said to Wyatt. "All right, Peter. I accept your proviso. We'll all go."

Andrew had been invited to have lunch with his school friend, Cortland, the next day, then go to a lecture at the Royal Archeological Society with Cortland and his grandfather, who was a member. As for Sara, she was very busy with her own affairs, for Verna took her to her own dressmaker on Albemarle Street to make sure she had exactly the right dress for the occasion.

The following day was cold but clear, and since Andrew and Sara had spent most of the previous day indoors, that afternoon they went skating on the pond in Regent's Park, only getting home in time for tea.

The reception was at ten o'clock at night, after an early performance at the Lyceum, so that the chosen of the London theatre world could attend. That meant that, after a light supper Sara could only pretend to eat, she and Andrew were supposed to rest until it was time to get dressed and go.

When they all met downstairs, Andrew had to admit that, considering the short time she'd had, Verna's Madam Viola had outdone herself. For the dress she had run up for Sara was of blue velvet with a lace collar and cuffs that made her look like the sister of Gainsborough's *Blue Boy*. Verna was wearing a dress that Andrew had seen before, but which he had always loved; a black lace dress, cut low in front and with a huge bow in back, that the great Worth himself had designed for her.

Andrew and Matson helped Verna and Sara on with their wraps, then they went out to the brougham that was waiting under the porte cochere. Since it was a cold night, Fred had prepared the warmers—heated bricks in the kitchen stove and put them in flannel sacks for them to put their feet on. Fred and Andrew covered the two ladies with a lap robe, Fred climbed up into the box and they were off.

Because of the lateness of the hour, there was very little traffic on the streets, and they made very good time.

The audience was just leaving the Savoy on the other side of the Strand when they drew up in front of the Lyceum, the theatre Henry Irving had made famous throughout the world.

Several constables stood under the marquee, scrutinizing each carriage as it drew up. Uniformed attendants helped them out of the brougham and ushered them into the lobby, which was even more brightly lit than it would have been before a performance. Another constable stood at the door with one of the theatre's staff who was checking off the names of the guests on a list he had in his hand. He knew Verna, bowed to her and waved her through into the theatre without asking her name.

They went down the central aisle of the orchestra, mounted the steps that had been installed so that they could get on to the stage, then followed the red carpet that had been laid down to the greenroom, which, in this theatre, was known as the Beefsteak Room. This too was a blaze of light with silver candlesticks on the side tables and other candles in the mirrored sconces as well as the usual gaslight.

Wyatt, elegant and completely unpolicemanlike in his evening clothes, stood at the entrance to the Beefsteak Room. Sergeant Tucker, in a sober dark suit, stood somewhat behind Wyatt and winked at Sara and Andrew when he saw them.

"My dear," said Wyatt, kissing the hand that Verna held out to him. "You look marvelous."

"So do you."

"I'm not supposed to. You are and you do. You know Mr. Irving?"

"Of course."

"Say hello to him and Miss Terry, have some champagne and circulate. I'll join you in a little while. As for you two," he said to Sara and Andrew, "you know what you have to do, don't you?"

"Yes," said Andrew, and Sara nodded wordlessly.

By now Henry Irving himself had seen Verna, and swept toward them.

"My dear Verna," he said, "how delighted I am to see you. This, I take it, is your son, Andrew, and your protégée, Miss Wiggins."

"Yes."

"I'm very happy to meet you both," he said, smiling at Sara who had dipped in a deep curtsey to him. "I know you know Miss Terry. Do take your son and Miss Wiggins over and introduce them to her."

Verna led them over to Ellen Terry, Irving's leading lady, who was of course as famous in her own right as he was. Andrew had seen her the previous season playing Portia in Irving's production of *The Merchant of Venice* and had admired her performance. Now, actually meeting her, he fell completely in love with her, as much for her easy and relaxed manner as for her looks.

She took them over to one of the long tables against the wall where caterer's men served food and drink and where she had them pour champagne for Verna and herself and ladle up cups of punch for Sara and Andrew. When she left them to greet a new arrival, Wyatt came toward them accompanied by a distinguished-looking man in his forties.

"My dear," he said, "I'd like to present someone who has long admired you. Felix Barnett. Verna Tillett."

Though Wyatt did not identify him further, Andrew and Sara knew at once that this must be the undersecretary of the Home Office. He bowed over Verna's hand, told her how moved he had been by her performance in *Jane Eyre*, went on to compare that with other roles she had played, and though Andrew had heard this sort of thing often before, he had to admit that Mr. Barnett not only spoke well and knowledgeably, but was probably sincere in his admiration. Verna introduced him to Sara, whom he charmed by remembering that she had been in *Jane Eyre* too and asking if she were going to be in anything else in the near future. He shook hands with Andrew, then returned his attention to Verna, asking questions about her new play and again showing a surprising amount of knowledge about it.

Wyatt, standing next to Verna, seemed very relaxed, nodding and smiling at acquaintances, but Andrew was aware of the tension under his casualness, noticed that his eyes were never still and that he took careful note of everything that was going on in the crowded room.

Sergeant Tucker stuck his head in for a moment, exchanging a look with Wyatt then disappearing again, and Wyatt said, "I think the guest of honor is arriving."

All those within earshot became silent and turned to face the door. Those who did not hear, sensing something, turned also, so that when the great actress appeared, everyone was waiting for her, looking at her, just as they would if she were making her entrance on stage.

She was tall and slender, and her pallor, as white and unblemished as an azalea, made her dark, deep-set eyes seem enormous. Her hair was dark brown with reddish lights in it. She wore a sea-green gown of watered silk that shimmered as she moved, so that she seemed not regal, but divine; some ancient goddess, translated there—to cold and foggy London—from the depths of a cobalt sea. She was followed by her own entourage: three men and two women, whom she completely ignored, never introduced.

She paused there in the doorway of the room. And seeing her, Irving and Ellen Terry hurried over to greet her as if she were royalty. And why shouldn't they when royalty itself treated her that way?

Bernhardt greeted them both with Gallic enthusiasm, embracing them in turn and chattering with them in a mixture of French and rudimentary English. Then, with Irving on one side of her and Ellen Terry on the other, they began the obligatory circling of the room to introduce her to those who merited an introduction.

Verna, of course, was one of the first to be so honored.

"I believe you know Verna Tillett, do you not?" said Irving.

"But of course," said Bernhardt in her throaty contralto. "We met when I was last here. My dear, you become younger and more beautiful every time I see you."

"If that's true," said Verna, "and of course I don't think it is—it's because I have been trying to follow the example you have given us."

"Do you hear her?" said Bernhardt, delighted. "As ready with *la phrase gentille* as if she had her own Shakespeare writing her lines! But who are these two?" she asked, looking at Sara and Andrew.

"This is my son, Andrew. And this is Sara Wiggins."

"Aha! You, my child, are an actress too, are you not?"

"I . . . well, I hope that some day I may be," said Sara. "But how did you know?"

"Because I have eyes, my dear. Besides, what would be the point of naming you after me if you were not to be an actress? What about you, Master Andrew? Are you interested in the theatre also?"

"Interested in it, but that's all. I mean, I don't think I could ever be an actor."

"Ah, well. We cannot all be on the boards. We need someone on the other side of the footlights for whom we can act our hearts out, *n'est-ce pas?*"

"Yes, madame."

"And these gentlemen?" said Bernhardt, looking at Wyatt and Mr. Barnett. Verna introduced them and, after looking at them appraisingly and approvingly, the great actress moved on, continuing her progress.

"Well, well," murmured Barnett. "No wonder they call her the divine Sarah."

"No wonder at all," said Wyatt, looking across the room. Something about the way he said it made Andrew turn and follow his gaze. Irving was introducing an attractive and sturdy-looking man to the guest of honor, and having only seen him once and then when he was dressed very casually, it took Andrew a moment to recognize Nicholas Norwood of the Golden Rule Society. He seemed to be as at home here with the great of the theatre world as he had been with the police and former criminals in The White Stag restaurant for he had a lengthy conversation with Madame Bernhardt, saying something to her that made her laugh delightedly and tap him on the arm in reproof.

Lawrence Harrison, the manager, and his wife came in now, and Verna introduced them to Mr. Barnett. While they were talking, Wyatt moved over to the bar where one of the waiters was pouring out a glass of champagne for Henry Irving.

"A very impressive, very successful reception, Mr. Irving."

"Why, thank you, Inspector. I think it's been going quite well myself." He paused, glancing around. "Is it all right to call you inspector? I know you're supposed to be more or less incognito . . ."

"It's quite all right. Anyone who knows me, knows who I am. As for strangers, if they should discover that I'm with the Yard, there's no reason for them to think that my presence here is anything but social."

"Quite true. And it doesn't hurt that you have so many good friends in and around the theatre—Verna Tillett and Larry Harrison. I was of course delighted to hear that you were going to be here yourself. After what has been happening, I must confess that I was a little concerned about Madame Bernhardt's safety."

"I can understand how you would be—especially since you're giving the reception for her. When did you first think of doing it?"

"About a month ago. I was having lunch with a friend, and when I said something about it—that I'd just learned that Bernhardt was going to be coming here—he suggested it."

"That you give a reception for her?"

"Yes. He's a great admirer of hers and was so taken with the idea of honoring her that he offered to foot the bill for it. But of course I told him that was un-necessary."

"Of course. Well, as I indicated, I think it was a splendid idea. Who was the friend who suggested it? Obviously someone in the theatre."

"Not really. Interested in it as any cultured Londoner is, but not actually in it. It was Nicholas Norwood. Do you know him?"

"Yes, of course. I couldn't think more highly of his Golden Rule Society. You say he's an old friend?"

"Yes. At least, I first met him quite a few years ago when he was still at Oxford. He was active in the Dramatic Society, and he got in touch with me and asked me whether I'd consider coming down and supervising their production of *The Merchant of Venice*."

"Which you did?"

"Yes. Very interesting production. I didn't see him for a number of years, but several months ago he got in touch with me again and . . . I'm sorry," he said, looking across the room. "Miss Terry seems to want me. Will you excuse me?"

"Of course," said Wyatt. He watched Irving walk over to Miss Terry, who was deep in conversation with Madame Bernhardt. Then he took a notebook out of his pocket, wrote something in it, tore out the page and, going over to the door, gave the note to Tucker. Tucker read it, nodded and went off to talk to one of the men, clearly a detective in plain clothes who was standing in the wings. A moment later Tucker was back and had resumed his post at the door where he could watch everything that was going on in the Beefsteak Room as well as in the whole backstage area.

Verna was talking to Lawrence Harrison and his

wife, and, though Andrew and Sara were with her, their eyes had been on Wyatt.

"What are you looking at?" he asked, walking over to them.

"Nothing," said Andrew.

"Since you were watching me, that's not very flattering."

"Isn't the fact that we *were* watching you and not Madame Bernhardt, Ellen Terry or Henry Irving flattery enough?" asked Sara.

"Of course, I wasn't serious."

"We know," said Andrew. It was obvious that Wyatt was up to something and he was dying to ask what it was, but he knew better than to ask. Harrison, however, had no such scruples.

"Any news?" he asked.

"About what?"

"Anything. With all due respects to our host and hostess, to the divine Sarah and, of course, Verna, you and your merry men are not here entirely because of your love and respect for the theatre."

"No, our primary job is to see that there *not* be any news. That nothing untoward happens."

"Of course. And so far, I must say you've done very well. Have you met our guest of honor?"

"For a moment—briefly."

"We'll have to see that you meet her again."

"I'd like that very much. What is it, Verna?" he asked as she shivered slightly.

"A sudden chill. It's not as warm back here as it might be."

"No, it's not," said Mrs. Harrison. "A door must be open somewhere. I feel a decided draft."

"Can I get you anything?" asked Andrew.

"Yes, dear. I think I'd like my shawl. I left it in the cloak room with my wrap."

As Andrew went off, Tucker came in from the door and gave Wyatt a note.

"Excuse me," he said. He read the note, nodded to Tucker, then turned back to the others. "I'm afraid I must ask you to excuse me again. May I speak to you for a moment, Verna?"

"Yes, of course, Peter." She followed him out of the Beefsteak Room. "What is it?"

"Something's come up—something important—and I've got to leave here for a while. I'd like you to come with me."

"You mean now—right now?"

"Yes."

"That's impossible!"

"Why is it impossible?"

"Because it is. You can't leave a reception like this that way, without thanking your host and hostess, saying goodbye to the guest of honor. And even if you gave me the time to do that . . ."

"I'm sorry," said Wyatt, grimly. "I don't have the time to argue with you about social graces or anything else." And he picked her up.

"Peter! What are you doing?"

Tucker came hurrying out of the dressing room that was being used as a cloak room carrying Verna's wrap and Wyatt's coat and hat.

"All right, Tucker. Forward!"

Carrying the astonished Verna in his arms, he followed Tucker to the stage door. Tucker opened it. There was a four-wheeler in the alley, a policeman in plain clothes in the box. Tucker opened the carriage door, and Wyatt got in, still carrying Verna.

"The upper end of Regent Street!" said Tucker. "And hurry!" Then throwing Verna's wrap and Wyatt's coat and hat into the carriage, he got in himself and slammed the door. The driver shook the reins, and the horse trotted up the alley, turned right on the Strand and, as the driver cracked his whip, went into a gallop.

12

The Caper

Andrew had just found Verna's things when Tucker hurried into the dressing room, grabbed them out of his hands and went hurrying out again. Taken aback, Andrew stood there for a moment, then went after him. He was in time to see Wyatt sweep Verna up in his arms, carry her out through the stage door and hear Tucker give his order to the plain clothes driver of the four-wheeler.

He was standing there, watching the carriage go up the alley and turn on to the Strand when Sara came up behind him.

"What was that about?" asked Andrew.

"What was what about?"

"What just happened. Tucker grabbed Mother's things away from me, Peter picked Mother up, carried her out the stage door, got into a carriage with her and away they went."

"Oh. Well, right after you went to get her shawl, Tucker came in and gave Peter a note. When he read it, he said he had to speak to her, and she went outside with him."

"I see." They looked at one another. "Something's up."

"Yes."

"I don't know what it is, but I know where they've gone."

"Where?"

"The upper end of Regent Street."

"Well, what are we waiting for?" asked Sara.

They got their things from the dressing room, ran out on to the stage, down through the theatre and the lobby to the Strand. The constables and uniformed attendants watched them go, but did not say anything to them. It was only when they reached the street that they paused to put on their coats. Fred was up the street, talking to two other coachmen, and didn't see them. Putting her fingers to her mouth, Sara whistled a shrill, street urchin's whistle, and Fred turned. They waved urgently to him, and unknotting the reins, he jumped into the box and brought the brougham down the street toward them.

"I assume you're going after the Inspector and Miss Tillett," said someone behind them.

They turned. It was Mr. Barnett, his white shirt front gleaming, for he had not stopped to pick up his coat.

"Yes, we are," said Andrew.

"Do you mind if I come with you?"

"Not at all." The brougham drew up, Andrew opened the door, motioned Sara and Mr. Barnett in and said to Fred, "This is the real thing, Fred. The inspector and Mother have just gone off to upper Regent Street, and we want to catch them. Can you do it?"

"If I can't, I won't be far behind them. Get in."

The carriage was moving before the door closed, precipitating Andrew into the back seat next to Sara.

"That was smartly done," said Barnett. "Your carriage?"

"Yes," said Andrew.

"Do either of you understand the purpose of this particular exercise?"

"I think so," said Sara. "The inspector just got a note. It probably told him that something he's been expecting has happened, and he thought he should be there."

"That sounds logical. But why did he take Miss Tillett with him?"

"Because he was worried about her," said Andrew. "You know what's happened to several actresses. He thought she might be in danger, and he wanted her with him so that he could watch over her, protect her."

"And that sounds logical, too. How did you know where they were going?"

"I heard Sergeant Tucker tell the driver who, I suspect, is a policeman."

"Simple enough, once it's been explained." Barnett looked at them in turn. "Sara Wiggins and Andrew Tillett. It seems to me I've heard about the two of you before this. Was it from my friend Chadwick in the Foreign Office?"

"It's possible. Young Chadwick is at school with me."

"I see. And then there was something to do with the Admiralty. The Cortland case."

"Cortland, Third, is a friend of mine, too."

"You seem to have some very interesting friends, including Inspector Wyatt. And"—looking out the window as they came into Trafalgar Square at a pelting gallop and turned north on Regent Street—"you also seem to have a very good coachman."

"He's the best there is in London," said Sara stoutly.

"He *is* good," said Andrew. "He used to be a jockey, and there aren't many coachmen who know horses and can handle them as well as Fred. In fact . . ." He put out an arm to brace himself and clutched Sara to keep her from pitching forward as the brougham came to a sudden, abrupt stop. "What's up, Fred?"

"This is as far as we can go. But there's the inspector."

Andrew opened the carriage door and jumped out, followed by Sara and Mr. Barnett. They were more than halfway up Regent Street, almost opposite Worthington's, the jeweler's. Directly in front of them, blocking the street, was a wooden barrier. A short distance beyond was the reason for the barrier—a roaring gas flame that burned furiously in a jet four to six feet high, lighting the whole of closed and shuttered Regent Street with its lurid, leaping light.

Wyatt and Tucker had gotten out of their four-wheeler, which had been stopped also, and Wyatt was talking to a uniformed policeman who stood on the far side of the barrier.

"What seems to be the trouble, Officer?" he asked.

"As you can see, sir. Broken gas main."

"Oh, yes," said Wyatt, looking at the burning jet. "Is there just the one break?"

"No, sir. There's another one further up Regent Street."

Looking up the street, Andrew and Sara could see another, similar flame burning at the upper end of Regent Street and effectively cutting it off from Oxford Street.

"Any idea how it happened?" asked Tucker.

"Some men were working here in the street—working after dark so as not to disrupt traffic—and they must have broken one of the mains."

"Is anything being done about it?" asked Barnett, going over to the barrier.

"Yes, sir," said the policeman, staring at his gleaming shirt front. "Inspectors from the gas company are down in one of the cellars looking for the valves that shut off the gas. But I must ask you to move on. You know how dangerous a gas leak is. There's always the danger of an explosion."

"You know, he's right, Wyatt," said Barnett, drawing back a little. "I think we should decamp forthwith."

"I agree," said Wyatt coolly and without turning around. "I think you should leave immediately. And take my young friends, who have no business here, along with you. Now then," he said to the police constable, "may I ask where you're attached?"

"What's that?"

"I asked you where you're attached. Are you with the Oxford Street Station or Piccadilly?"

"Oxford Street, but—" He jumped as there was a muffled but decided explosion somewhere that rattled all the windows on Regent Street. "There! Did you hear that? I told you it was dangerous! Now will you get out of here?"

"Oh, I will eventually," said Wyatt. "But not quite yet."

"I must say I don't understand this, Wyatt," said

Barnett uneasily. "If you're not concerned about your own safety, you should be about Miss Tillett's."

"But I am, Mr. Barnett. Very concerned. That's why I have her with me. As for you, I told you to get along. If you'll go back to the Lyceum, we'll be returning there ourselves fairly soon, and . . . Ah! There we are," he said as two men in the caps and uniforms of gas company inspectors came hurrying out of Worthington's carrying lanterns and bags of tools. "Are these the men from the gas company, Officer?"

"Yes, sir. They are."

"All right, Sergeant."

Whipping out his whistle, Tucker blew a shrill blast on it. Immediately ten to a dozen men, some in police uniform but most of them in plain clothes, appeared from the darkness of the side streets and from dark shops that had seemed to be closed.

The two men in the gas company uniforms tried to run but were collared almost immediately. One of them lost his cap, and when he turned around to pick it up, Andrew saw that he was Nifty Bolan.

"We'll want the two fake cops as well as the gas inspectors," said Wyatt. "And there's somebody over there, hiding in that alley, that I'd like to take a look at."

Whistling again, Tucker pointed, and one of the uniformed policemen dived into a narrow alley between a chemist's and a stationer's and dragged out another figure who looked familiar.

"Why, it's Mr. Collins!" said Sara as the constable brought him out into the flaring yellow light of the gas jet.

"Suppose it is," said the old stage carpenter angrily. "Is it agin' the law just to be out in the street at night?"

"No, Mr. Collins," said Wyatt.

"Then why are you putting the nab on me? I ain't done nothing!"

"Are you saying you had nothing to do with this very interesting performance here—the supposedly broken gas mains?"

"I ain't saying nothing about nothing!"

"I'm sorry to hear that. I hope I can persuade you that it might be to your interest to say quite a good deal about several things. Bring him along too, Tucker."

"I'm sorry. I'm completely at a loss," said Barnett. "You seem to know what's going on, and I trust you'll explain, but . . . May I ask where we're going?"

"Where I told you to go—back to the Lyceum. In the first place we left quite abruptly, without thanking our host and hostess or saying goodbye. And, in the second place, you did give me the responsibility for Madame Bernhardt's safety as well as Miss Tillett's."

13

Flowers for a Leading Lady

The porter of the Oxford and Cambridge Club sat up with a start. Then, when the night bell rang again, even more loudly and insistently, he went to the door and peered out toward Pall Mall. A cab waited there and a man in a bowler hat stood outside the door, tapping his foot impatiently. The porter didn't know him, but he looked quite respectable so, when he raised his hand to ring for the third time, the porter opened the door a few inches.

"Yes, sir?" he said. "Can I help you?"

"Yes," said the man. "You can let me in."

"I beg your pardon. Are you a member of the club, sir?"

"No, I'm not. But I'm a member of the Metropolitan Police. Here's my identification." He held up his warrant card.

"The police? Do you know where you are?"

"Of course I know. And I also know what time it is, so let's not go into that. Now are you going to let me in or not?"

"What is it, Parker?" asked the club steward, coming down the corridor from the billiard room.

"Someone from the police. He wants to come in, and . . ."

"Sorry to bother you, sir," said the man. "I know it's late, but it's very important. Here's my card."

"Detective Sergeant Thatcher," said the steward, looking at it.

"Yes, sir. While I'm not a member of the club, I was sent here by Inspector Wyatt who is. He needs some information, which he thinks you can find in your library."

"Yes, I know Inspector Wyatt," said the steward. "Let him in, Parker. Now what is this information he wants?"

"It's written out here, sir," said the sergeant, handing him the note Wyatt had given Tucker.

"Hmm," said the steward, reading it. "Come along to the library with me, Sergeant, and I'll see if I can find it for you."

Meanwhile, back at the theatre, things had not worked out quite the way Wyatt had expected. Anx-

ious to cause as little comment—and as little distur-
bance—as possible, he had led the police in by way of
the stage door. They found the Beefsteak Room almost
completely empty. Only one or two guests remained
there, having a last glass of champagne before they left.

Henry Irving, who had been on his way out, heard
the stage door open and came back accompanied by
Nicholas Norwood.

"Oh, it's you, Inspector. We were wondering
where you'd gone."

"Something came up—something I had to look
into—and I took the liberty of taking Miss Tillett with
me."

"We thought it must be something like that. I'm
afraid our festivities have more or less come to an end.
Though of course you're welcome to stay on here for
as long as you like."

"Thank you. We may just do that until we get a
few things sorted out. I take it Madame Bernhardt
has gone then?"

"She's just leaving. Her people and Miss Terry are
waiting outside for Norwood and me, and we're all
going to her hotel for a nightcap. Though I don't see
any need for it, three of your men have insisted on
accompanying us."

"Quite right. Don't you agree, Mr. Barnett?"

"I do. Commissioner's orders."

"Well, if you think it's absolutely necessary . . . Coming, Norwood?"

"I don't know," said Norwood, who had been looking past Wyatt at the small group of men—Bolan, Collins and the two fake policemen—who stood in the background, watched by Sergeant Tucker and several of his colleagues. "Is that Bolan there?"

"It is."

"What's he doing here? Is he under arrest?"

"He is."

"Who's Bolan?" asked Henry Irving.

"A protégé of mine—or rather of the Society," said Norwood. "Someone I tried to help. And if he's gotten himself into trouble, I think I should stand by."

"Oh, absolutely. If he's a protégé of yours, it must be a misunderstanding. We'll run along, and you can join us at the hotel later on."

"Right. Do you mind if I stay, Inspector?"

"Not at all. Glad to have you," said Wyatt. He nodded to Tucker, who started bringing out chairs for Verna, Sara and Andrew, while one of the constables brought some out for Bolan, Collins and the others.

"Why is he dressed that way?" asked Norwood, frowning at Bolan, who resolutely avoided his eyes. "And what's he charged with?"

"He's dressed that way because he's impersonating

an inspector for the Metropolitan Gas Company," said Wyatt. "As to the reason for it, that's rather complicated. However, if you'll be patient—" He broke off as the stage door opened and closed again. "See who that is, Sergeant," he said to Tucker.

But Tucker had gone out even before he was told to investigate and came back almost immediately.

"It's that boy from Foljamb's," he said. "With some flowers."

"That's who it is," said Happy Jack, appearing in the doorway with an enormous box of flowers. "The boy from Foljamb's." He paused for a moment, leaning on his crutch. "Well, well. Lot of old friends here tonight," he said, looking at Sara and Andrew. "*And* a relative," he said, looking at his grandfather. "But I don't see the person I came to see."

"Who's that?" asked Wyatt.

"The great Madame Bernhardt. The divine Sarah. That's who the flowers is for. Don't tell me she's gone!"

"I'm afraid she has," said Wyatt.

"Oh, no! I told Mr. Foljamb I shouldn't wait until too late, but he wouldn't listen to me. 'Late's better than early,' he said, and he's the boss; so I did what he said, and you can see what happened. But still," he said, looking across the room with shining eyes, "all is not lost. There's someone else here I can give the flowers to—someone I think is just as divine as the French lady." Swinging forward smoothly on his crutch, he started across the room toward Verna.

Suddenly—and without really knowing why—Andrew became anxious. It may have been because of Happy Jack's unnatural pallor, the gleam in his eye and the smile that wasn't truly a smile. Whatever the reason, all at once he didn't want Jack to go anywhere near his mother. But even as he started forward, old Mr. Collins said, "No, Jack! No!" and Wyatt stepped in front of Verna.

"I'll take the flowers, Jack," he said.

Jack paused. "What?"

"I said, I'll take the flowers."

"No, no," said Jack, shaking his head. "Can't do that. Got to give them to her myself."

"Well, you can't," said Wyatt flatly.

"Why are you being so difficult, Peter?" asked Verna. "The boy's not doing anyone any harm."

"Isn't he?"

"No. He's just . . ." She gasped as Jack suddenly raised his crutch and drove the tip at Wyatt's throat. Wyatt pushed it aside, and it hit his shoulder instead of his throat. There was a metallic click, and Wyatt staggered back with blood staining his shoulder. Pulling back the crutch, which now had a needlelike spike projecting from the tip, Jack was about to stab Wyatt with it again when, with a diving tackle, Andrew knocked him to the ground.

With surprising speed, Jack picked up the crutch, which Andrew had knocked from his hands, and was struggling to his feet when Sergeant Tucker reached him and, lifting him up, pinioned his arms behind him.

"Peter, are you all right?" asked Verna, her face white.

"Yes," said Wyatt.

"Let me see," said Verna, helping him off with his jacket and looking at the stab wound in his shoulder. "Andrew, give me your handkerchief."

He handed it to her, and she folded it and placed it as a pad on the wound.

"I don't understand," said Sara as Verna, working swiftly and efficiently, tore a long strip from the bottom of her petticoat and began to bandage Wyatt's shoulder. "You mean it was him . . . Jack . . ."

"Yes," said Jack, twisting and pulling in Tucker's grip. "It was me . . . me . . . me that done it, done them in. And I only wish I'd had a chance to do more of 'em before you got me!"

"But why?"

"You want to know why? I'll tell you! You really think they called me Happy Jack like I said they did? Happy?" He snorted. "*Hoppy* Jack is what they called me—hoppy, like a frog! 'Come on, Jack. Let's see you hop!' and they'd knock me down or throw things at me till I hopped like they wanted me to! And afterwards, after I left the raggedy school, it was even worse! How do you think I felt about you, all of you who was so straight and could skip and run and jump and all when I was so twisted and could hardly walk? I hated you—hated you 'specially when you looked at me so kind and pitying like, feeling so sorry for me! But most of all I hated *them!*" he said, spitting at Verna. "Actresses!"

"Why, Jack?" asked Wyatt quietly.

"Because they killed me mum, one of them did, and made me this way!"

"Who's 'they,' Jack? Who did it? And how?"

"I don't know who. They was all jealous of her, all of them! As to how . . . They left a stage trapdoor open and she fell through it, fell into the basement. It was just before I was born, and it killed her and made me the way I am, all twisted up."

"And what was your mother's name? Was it Sally Siddons?"

"Yes, it was."

Wyatt looked at old Mr. Collins, who was bent forward and holding his head.

"She was your daughter, wasn't she, Mr. Collins?"

"Yes."

"Is what Jack said the truth?"

"No, it's not."

"What do you mean, it's not the truth?" said Jack. "She told me it was!"

"Who's 'she'?" asked Wyatt. "Your mother?"

"No. That other woman—the one I met a couple of weeks ago. She was my friend, and she said she'd tell me things my gramps had never told me."

"Who was this woman? What was her name?"

"I don't know. She never told me her name. She used to meet me when I was leaving Foljamb's and walk with me, talk to me. All I know about her is that she was a real lady, spoke like a lady."

"Do you know who that lady was, Mr. Collins?"

"No," he said. But it seemed to Andrew that he hesitated for a fraction of a second before he said it, and he got the feeling that Wyatt had noticed it, too.

"You never spoke to her, had any dealings with her?"

"Maybe I did, but I don't know who she was."

"All right. We'll come back to that. But what about what Jack just told us?"

"He was born the way he is, all crooked like, and not because Sally fell through any trapdoor. She never did fall through any trapdoor, didn't die that way."

"But it did happen that way. It did!" shrieked Jack. "That woman told me it did!"

"If it happened before you were born and killed her," said Wyatt, "how is it that it didn't kill you?"

"What? I don't know. Maybe it didn't kill her right away. Maybe she just got hurt and died after I was born."

"No," said Collins. "The birthing woman—midwife

—what helped bring you said it happened like that sometimes: a baby born all crookedy. She said it was a kind of sickness."

"No!" said Jack, jerking upright and starting to tremble. "You're lying! You're all lying! *They* did it to her—actresses—because they was all jealous of her! The lady told me—that's why I did what I did! And I know it's true! It's got to be true! If it's not . . ." He suddenly groaned, his eyes rolled up and he sagged and would have fallen to the floor if Tucker had not held him up.

"Fainted," said Tucker. "Looks to me like he might get fits."

"Yes," said Wyatt. "I want a doctor to look at him. Have him taken to the French Hospital—that's the nearest one—and make sure someone stays with him, watches him, until I get over there."

He signaled to two constables, who took the unconscious boy and went off with him.

"What about you, Inspector?" said Tucker. "Don't you want a doctor to look at your shoulder?"

"Later. We've got too much to do now, and it seems to have stopped bleeding." He picked up the crutch that Jack had dropped. "How does this work?" he asked Collins.

"There's a spring inside the crutch. If you bear down on the needle, it'll go up inside and a catch will hold it." Wyatt pressed the tip of the needle to the floor, and it disappeared up inside the crutch, catching with a click.

"How do you release it?"

"That little knob halfway down where you grip it."

Wyatt pressed the knob, and the needle sprang out again.

"Very ingenious. You made it, didn't you?"

"Yes."

"And gave it to Jack?"

"No, I didn't give it to him. He found it and took it. He said he wanted it to protect himself against boys who had been bullying him, beating him."

"And you believed him?"

"Why not? Before he had the crutch, he'd sometime come home with a black eye, hurt and bruised."

"And what about those recent deaths? Didn't you wonder about them?"

"Why should I? The papers never said how they'd been killed. It never dawned on me that maybe Jack had done it—if he really did."

"What do you mean, if he really did? You heard him say he had committed the murders!"

"Well, yes," said Collins awkwardly. "But he's not quite right in the head—never has been."

"All right. Let's go back ten years or so. You made the crutch for your daughter, Sally, didn't you?"

"No, I didn't."

"You didn't make it? You just said you did."

"I made it, but not for her. I made it as a prop for a play—*The Crooked Man From Crewe*—where this mad doctor uses it to kill people."

"I don't remember any such play," said Wyatt. "Do you?" he asked Verna.

"No."

"It never opened. That's why I still had the crutch. Ben Green was supposed to play the part, but he decided he didn't like it and backed out, and the play was dropped."

"It should be easy enough to check that. For whatever reason, you made the crutch. How did your daughter, Sally, get hold of it?"

"She . . . she took it."

"Just took it? Why?"

"She . . . she hurt her ankle, needed something to help her walk, so she took it."

"You mean, that's what she said."

"Yes."

"And didn't you realize later on what she really wanted it for? That she used it to kill three actresses?"

"No, no! I didn't know it! I never knew how they died—no one did—so I never thought she might have done it!"

"Even though she was very close to Ben Wallace, expected to play the lead in his pantomime? And expected it because he was the father of her child?"

"That . . . that had nothing to do with it. He died of heart failure."

"Yes, when he realized that Sally had killed his wife. Killed her because she was jealous of her, and because she thought—if you can call it thinking—that when his wife was dead, she'd get her part in the pantomime."

"It's not true," whispered Collins weakly. "It's not."

"I don't want to interfere, Inspector," said Barnett, "but I'd like to make sure I understand this. Are you saying that this man's daughter—that sick boy's mother—was responsible for the deaths of those actresses some ten years ago?"

"I am. I think she killed Nina Wallace for the reason I gave. She killed Aggie Russell, Nina's friend, because she was the only person who knew that Sally had gone to see Nina. And she committed a third murder in order to disguise the motive for the other two."

"And where is she, this woman?"

"She's dead, isn't she, Mr. Collins?"

"Yes. Went to Canada right after Jack was born, leaving me to take care of him. She tried to act there and in the States, but couldn't get no parts and finally got sick and died."

"Then no matter what your suspicions are, Inspector," said Barnett, "there's no point in your trying to prove it."

"No."

"How does all this relate to that unfortunate Jack boy? I gather you think there was something mentally wrong with his mother. There's certainly something wrong with him. And if there is—if he's mentally backward—how was he able to determine what his mother had done and, no matter what his sick motive was, decide to do the same thing himself?"

"He didn't. Someone told him that completely fabricated story about his mother's fall through the trapdoor and his supposed injury in order to give him a motive. And then went on to tell him what to do about it, how to use the crutch as she had done."

"But who could have done such a thing? And why?"

"Those are two very interesting questions. Let's take the second one first."

"Forgive me, Inspector," said Mr. Norwood, who had been following everything that had been said with fascination. "When I asked if I could stay here, I didn't realize that you were going into anything quite so elaborate and complicated. You know what my interest is."

"Yes. Your client or protégé—or rather that of your estimable Golden Rule Society—Mr. Nifty Bolan. We're just going to get to him. And get to him by way of Mr. Collins. Would you care to tell us, Mr. Collins, what you were doing on Regent Street this evening?"

"What?" said Collins heavily. "Look, I'm not feeling so good. I don't want to talk about it."

"I'm afraid you may have to. You were the one who arranged it, weren't you? The supposedly broken gas mains, the flames and all that?"

"All right. Yes, I did. It was harder to do than a transformation in panto because I didn't have no stage to work with, but I did it. What are you going to charge me with on that?"

"That depends," said Wyatt.

"But what was the purpose of it?" asked Barnett. "Unless..." His eyes widened. "Was it robbery?"

"Of course. Everything that happened tonight—everything that's been happening for some time—has been part of an elaborate plot to crack the richest crib in London. Sergeant," he said to Tucker, "could we take a look at what Bolan had in that bag when we nabbed him?"

"This one, sir?" asked one of the constables holding up an old carpet bag.

"No, no. We know what's in that. The burglar tools that Mr. Collins sharpened and put in shape for Bolan. The other one."

The constable handed Tucker a gunny sack. Reaching into it, Tucker took out several large, velvet-covered cases, which he handed to his chief. Wyatt opened one, held it up, and they all gasped, for it blazed with the light of the jewels it contained: a wide, elaborate necklace of diamonds, rubies and emeralds.

"The Ghazipur jewels!" whispered Barnett.

"*And* anything else that might be easily available in Worthington's vaults."

"I must say I'm impressed, Inspector," said Barnett. "You seem to have solved two sets of murders and prevented what would probably have been the greatest robbery of our time."

"I can't say I understand everything that you've said, Inspector," said Norwood, "everything that's been going on, but I agree with Mr. Barnett and congratulate you also. And this in spite of the fact that you have caused me great distress. Because, as I said before, Bolan there is a protégé of mine. Or at least, of the Golden Rule Society. But now . . . Is he the man who's responsible for what I gather was a very elaborate plot?"

"It certainly was elaborate. Are you clear on just how it was supposed to work?" Wyatt asked Barnett.

"I'm not sure I am. At least, I'm not certain I understand how the murders fit it."

"They were an important part of the plan. Their purpose was to stir up the press and the public so that the police would concentrate their attention and most of their strength here in the theatre district at the time when the robbery was to be attempted elsewhere. And of course the whole performance was carefully orchestrated, and the night picked for the attempt was the night when—not only most of our own great actresses—but a great visiting actress, Madame Bernhardt, was to be here and possibly vulnerable. But to answer Mr. Norwood's question. No. Nifty Bolan, who is just a cracksman, was only a tool and not the intelligence behind this very well worked-out plan."

"But who was behind it?" asked Barnett. "Do you know?"

"Yes, I do. I had only a suspicion until tonight, but now I believe I can prove it." He glanced over at the entrance to the Beefsteak Room, and Andrew and Sara saw that Beasley, wearing a bowler and a dark coat, had come in and was standing behind the constables who guarded the door.

"And who is it? Are you going to tell us?" asked Barnett.

"Why, yes. I intend to."

"Is it all right for me to stay?" asked Norwood. "I have a feeling that my presence here is rather irregular. Though I suspect that the whole proceeding is irregular."

"Indeed it is, Mr. Norwood. And I have no objection whatsoever to your staying. As to whom the man behind the plot is—the Napoleon of crime about whom I spoke to you the other day, Mr. Barnett—I'd like to remind you of the person Happy Jack said had told him that wild story about his mother, the story that turned him into a murderer."

"As I recall, all he said was that it was a woman."

"Exactly. And who was it that approached you, Mr. Collins, and had you arrange that little performance with the gas jets on Regent Street?"

"It was a woman. I never got a good look at her 'cause I only talked to her in the dark. And I never talked about it to Jack, but now I got a feeling it was probably the same one that talked to him."

"Now let's get to you, Bolan. You were caught with the goods, and with your record, you're going to be up for quite a stretch. However, we might be willing to talk up for you if you'll tell us what we want to know. Who put you up to the job?"

"I don't know," said Bolan. "Like Dabby Dick Collins there, I never got a good look at her 'cause I only seen her in the dark, but . . ."

"But you too say that the person who approached you, told you what to do and how to do it, was a woman."

"That's right, guv'ner."

"Well, as I said, though I had my suspicions, I had no way of proving what I thought until this evening when a new fact came to my attention. I asked Mr. Henry Irving how and when he got the idea of having

the reception for Madame Bernhardt, and he said that
the idea had been suggested to him by someone else:
his friend, Mr. Norwood. Is that true, Mr. Norwood?"

"Yes, it is. I've been an admirer of Madame Bernhardt's for a long time."

"You are, of course, not alone there. Then I asked
Mr. Irving if you had been friends for a long time, and
he said you had been for quite a few years. Ever since
you, Mr. Norwood, were at Oxford."

"That's true. I was with the Oxford Dramatic Society. Mr. Irving had just put on his memorable production of *The Merchant of Venice*, and as secretary
of the society, I wrote and asked him if he would come
down and supervise our production of the same play."

"Yes. The only thing I did not know at the time—
did not know, in fact, until I sent someone over to the
Oxford and Cambridge Club to look the matter up—
was that you yourself had been in that production of
The Merchant of Venice—playing the part of Portia!
More than that, that most of the roles you played at
Oxford were women!"

There was dead silence for a moment.

"Are you suggesting . . . implying . . ." began
Barnett.

"I am not implying or suggesting. I am saying flatly
that Mr. Nicholas Norwood was the man who got
that poor, misguided boy, Jack, to commit those murders—who planned the whole elaborate robbery at-

tempt on Regent Street tonight and engaged both Bolan and Collins to take part in it!"

"And you base all this on the fact that I played some women's roles while I was at Oxford?" said Norwood. "Really, Inspector . . ."

"No, Mr. Norwood. I base it on a lot more than that. But I see that an old friend of mine has just arrived. Did you want to see me, Mr. Beasley?"

"Yes, I did, Inspector," said Beasley, taking off his bowler and speaking with great formality. "Something rather interesting happened a short while ago, and since you informed me that you'd be here, I thought I'd come by and tell you about it."

"Tell me what, Mr. Beasley?"

"Well, I was walking through Carnaby Street in Soho when suddenly there was this kind of shlemozzle, not to say shindig, up ahead of me. Seems like someone had broken into an office somewhere around there, and a copper had come along and spotted it. The boyo that had done the breaking in scarpered, with the cop running after him and blowing on his whistle, and like a good citizen, I ran after them. Then suddenly the chap that was running dropped something, and I picked it up. It turned out to be a book."

"What kind of a book?" asked Wyatt.

"A notebook," said Beasley. "And since it was probably stolen, I thought maybe I should turn it over to you, and—"

"Let me see that!" said Norwood as Beasley handed Wyatt a small black notebook.

"Why?" asked Wyatt with apparent innocence. "Do you think it might be yours?"

"Well, as you know, the office of the Golden Rule Society is on Carnaby Street."

"I know it is. And I think this probably *is* your notebook. It seems to be in code, and I suspect it's the key to another book in your office: a book that lists all the criminals that your society has had dealings with. That one would tell you what their skills are and whether they're amenable to doing a little work for a mysterious, unknown woman—like opening the safe at Worthington's."

"That's ridiculous! You'll never be able to prove that!"

"When we decipher the code in this little notebook, which I'm sure we'll be able to do, I think we will be able to prove it."

"What you're saying, Inspector," said Barnett," is that while Mr. Norwood appeared to be helping to reform criminals by getting them legitimate employment, he was actually building up a secret roster of criminal talents."

"That's correct."

"It's certainly an ingenious idea. Though it may be, as Mr. Norwood insists, a little difficult to prove. On the other hand, there doesn't seem to be any doubt that you discovered who was responsible for those frightful deaths or, as I said, that you kept the Ghazipur jewels from being stolen."

"I did. But not quite in the way you think."

"I beg your pardon?"

"They were never in any real danger because those jewels there, the ones that were taken from Worthington's vault, are not the real jewels at all. They're copies."

"What? But how did you know that there would be an attempt to steal them?"

"I didn't *know* that there would be, but I suspected that there might be and worked out the precautions with Worthington's and another jeweler, informing the press that Worthington's had them, while they were actually elsewhere. This was a necessary measure if we were to set the trap we did, pretending that we were so concerned about Madame Bernhardt and the other actresses here that we were forgetting about the jewels."

"So he really did you in the eye, didn't he, you sodding toff!" said Bolan to Norwood. "Even if we'd pulled it off, it wouldn't have done us no good!"

"Are you admitting that you know him now, Bolan?" said Wyatt. "That you realize he was the woman who arranged for you to rob Worthington's?"

"No, but I'm sure that he was—all that mealy-mouthed talk about going straight—"

"Shut up, you fool!" said Norwood furiously. "Don't you know when to keep your mouth shut?"

"Well, well," said Barnett. "What do they say happens when thieves fall out?" Then, looking more closely at Wyatt. "My dear fellow, are you all right? You're suddenly looking very seedy!"

"I am feeling a bit rocky," said Wyatt.

"I'm taking you to have that shoulder looked at!" said Verna firmly. "Sergeant Tucker, can you take over with whatever has to be done with these men?"

"I can and will," said Tucker. "All right, boys. Off to the nick with them so we can book them proper."

"We're going to need Fred and the carriage," said Verna to Beasley, as Tucker and his colleagues began leading off Norwood, Bolan and the others. "Could you see that Sara and Andrew get home safely?"

"I'll be glad to do that," said Mr. Barnett.

"No, sir," said Beasley. "With all due respect, I've known them longer than you have, and I claim the privilege. Come on, young 'uns."

"So, as usual, you were in the whole thing from the start, weren't you?" said Sara as they left the Beefsteak Room.

"What makes you say that?" said Beasley.

"You must have been," said Andrew. "You got Clipson to go see Norwood—I gather because Peter asked you to—which means that he must have been a little suspicious of Norwood for some time. And now that I think of it, I finally understand something that always puzzled me."

"I'll bet I know what it is," said Sara. "Was it that business with the safe in Norwood's office?"

"Yes. Of course there was nothing wrong with it. It was kind of a test Norwood had made up so he could be sure he was getting a really good cracksman for that Regent Street job."

"I wouldn't know about that," said Beasley.

"No?" said Sara. "Then let me ask you about something else. What were you doing on Carnaby Street?"

"What do you usually do there? I'd gone shopping with a friend."

"At eleven o'clock at night?" said Andrew.

"Not an ideal time, I grant you, but I don't have much choice. After all, I've got a shop of my own that I have to keep open."

"Of course," said Sara. "All right. Then who was the friend you went shopping with? Could it have been Keegee Clipson, who'd been to the Golden Rule Society office once already and can pick a lock as easy as kiss me?"

"Are you suggesting that Keegee broke into the Golden Rule office and *stole* that book?"

"Did he?"

"My dear Miss Wiggins, I'm shocked—absolutely

shocked—that you could even think such a thing! Do you realize that it would be not only illegal but unethical?"

"I suppose it would be."

"All right. Then may I urge you to stow your gob before someone who doesn't know me as well as you do overhears you?"